THE BODY IN QUESTION

THE BODY IN QUESTION

a novel by

Jill Ciment

PANTHEON BOOKS   NEW YORK

All rights reserved. Published in the United States by Pantheon Books,
a division of Penguin Random House LLC, New York, and distributed
in Canada by Random House of Canada, a division of Penguin
Random House Canada Limited, Toronto.

Pantheon Books and colophon are registered trademarks of Penguin
Random House LLC.

Grateful acknowledgment is made to the following for permission to reprint
previously published material:

Grove/Atlantic, Inc.: Excerpts from *Eleven* by Patricia Highsmith,
copyright © 1945, 1962, 1964, 1965, 1967, 1968, 1969, 1970 by Patricia
Highsmith. Reprinted by permission of Grove/Atlantic, Inc. Any third
party use of this material, outside of this publication, is prohibited.

W. W. Norton & Company, Inc.: Excerpt of "Touch Me" from
Passing Through: The Later Poems New and Selected by Stanley Kunitz,
copyright © 1995 by Stanley Kunitz. Reprinted by permission of
W. W. Norton & Company, Inc.

Library of Congress Cataloging-in-Publication Data
Name: Ciment, Jill, [date] author.
Title: The body in question : a novel / Jill Ciment.
Description: First Edition. New York : Pantheon Books, 2019.
Identifiers: LCCN 2018037798.
ISBN 9781524747985 (hardcover : alk. paper).
ISBN 9780525565376 (ebook).
Subjects: GSAFD: Suspense fiction.
Classification: LCC PR9199.3.C499 B63 2019 | DDC 813/.54—dc23 |
LC record available at lccn.loc.gov/2018037798

www.pantheonbooks.com

Jacket illustration by Cody Comrie
Jacket design by Janet Hansen

Printed in the United States of America
First Edition
2 4 6 8 9 7 5 3 1

In Memory of Arnold

What makes the engine go?
Desire, desire, desire.

—Stanley Kunitz, "Touch Me"

Part One

W hen that door opens, sign out. Say you're taking a cigarette break," he says.

"I don't smoke," she says.

"You don't have to smoke, just sign out. If they call your number,
ignore them."

Neither notices the door open.

"A friend of mine got out just by saying he couldn't sit under the
words 'In God We Trust,'" she says.

Her number is called, C-2.

"You have another angle?" she asks.

"If one of the lawyers asks if you've ever been involved with an
attorney, tell him he picked you up in a bar five years ago."

"You're assuming the lawyer will be a man," she says.

"Tell her she picked you up in a Lowe's five years ago. She had
the power sander, you had the tool belt."

The second time her number is called, she rises reluctantly.

"Hey," he calls after her as she makes her way between the uneven
rows of folding chairs. "Good luck."

C-2 is surprised to find the courtroom already in session. Everyone but the defendant, a girl in her late teens, looks up as C-2 takes the only empty chair in the jury box. The other five chairs are occupied by women of varying ages. Three sport flip-flops. One is dressed as if for a hot date. One wears church clothes.

The judge, an older African American woman with a no-nonsense haircut, asks the defendant to turn around in her chair and face the prospective jurors. The defendant's head revolves so slowly that C-2 can't discern whether the sluggishness is deliberate, to arrest the court's attention, or if the teenager in the ill-fitting but very expensive clothes has something physically or mentally wrong with her. Her most striking feature is her hair: the bottom six inches are dyed shoe-polish black, the top six inches are Barbie blond.

C-2 has studied her share of faces. She started her career as a portrait photographer for *Rolling Stone* and *Interview* magazine until it finally sank in: she wasn't interested in people. As individuals. She was interested in them as a species.

The defendant's features are the kind found in how-to-draw books—sketchy and basic. If C-2 were to close her eyes, she doubts she would remember what is inside the blank oval a second later.

If C-2 had to wager a guess as to the teenager's crime, she would bet shoplifting, or selling her grandmother's Percocets to her classmates, or both. A one- or two-day trial at most.

The judge asks, "Do any of you recognize the defendant?"

Two hands shoot up.

"I saw her on TV," says one of the flip-flop set.

"On Court TV," says the woman who has removed her lip and nose rings out of respect for court.

The defendant's counsel, a full-figured woman in her early thirties, and the jury consultant, a gray-haired gentleman in Armani, confer: the two women are dismissed. Two more potential jurors enter the court and take the vacated chairs: a woman who looks pregnant but is too old to be pregnant, and the young man with whom C-2 had been mildly flirting in the holding area—in his early forties, whereas C-2 is fifty-two—the one who had all the clever answers on how to get out of jury duty. He catches her attention and shrugs self-mockingly. His eyes are a blue that seems too crystalline to belong to his face, which is pitted with acne scars. Other than the church lady, he is the only one dressed appropriately for court; khakis, white shirt, closed shoes. C-2 is wearing cutoffs and a T-shirt. It is 95 degrees outside.

"This is a murder trial," the judge says.

The defendant slides her eyes sideways in her expressionless face. C-2 follows the stare. It lands on a middle-aged woman seated in the front row of the gallery, her face an illustration of anguish. A blond replica of the defendant comforts the woman, but this version is prettier. Her face is vibrant, as if each feature were an individual puppet and she were the puppet master. If C-2 closed her eyes, she would remember that face.

"The trial may take up to three weeks," the judge explains, "and may involve sequestration. Is there anyone who believes themselves incapable of fulfilling such an obligation?"

C-2's standby excuse, that she couldn't sit under "In God We Trust," seems flippant, almost reprehensible to use given that the middle-aged woman is shuddering and imploding in the gallery. C-2 could tell the judge that her husband is eighty-six, the truth, and that she is his sole caretaker, her fear.

The woman too old to be pregnant and the man with the lucent blue eyes raise their hands.

"F-17," the man introduces himself to the judge. "I'm a professor at the medical school. My Gross Anatomy course begins next week. I have twenty-one cadavers waiting for me."

"Aren't they already dead?" the judge asks.

Again that self-mocking shrug. "Yes," he says.

"They can wait."

The woman's hand is still up. "J-12. I'm going in for tests next week," she says.

The judge waits a beat for anyone else to speak up.

C-2 could still raise her hand. Though her husband retains his impressive, curious mind, he loses things daily—keys, words, height, mass, the ability to hear conversations, his peripheral vision (though he insists on still driving), the subtlety of taste, and the assault of smell. And most alarming, the loss of the sixth sense, proprioception, the ability to know the position of one's body parts. Her husband isn't always sure where his hands and feet are without having to look for them. It takes him a wooden moment to reach for things, to make those measurements one unconsciously calculates each time one dips under a low beam, or eats popcorn in the dark. He can still navigate the day's obstacles, but for how much longer? C-2 is becoming his copilot. Her senses must work double-time shepherding two separate bodies through space, but to refuse the job—not to point out the broken step, not to repeat the punch line he couldn't hear—will mean abandoning him in the woolly, dim, mute isolation of old age.

She met her husband when she was twenty-four and he was fifty-seven. He was a Pulitzer-winning journalist and she had just given up portraiture for something more dangerous. He had asked her to be his photographer on an assignment in El Salvador—civil war had broken out yet again. He had flown first-class, and she had flown economy. Not once during the seven-hour flight did he venture back into steerage to see how she was faring. That had cinched it for her: her attraction for him was an unreciprocated crush; he had only been interested in her photography.

At the San Salvador airport, they hitched a prearranged ride in a bus chartered by Hollywood's radical chic, a director of conspiracy thrillers, an earnest actress, and her producer husband. The actress had come to interview the charming mustachioed general of the rebels. The van had to cross the mountains before nightfall and curfew. The road was a stretch of graveled ascent, bracketed with makeshift checkpoints manned by ragged boys with rifles.

The producer broke out a bottle of Valium and handed the pills around. C-2 noted that the war correspondent didn't take one, so she didn't either, even though she wanted one very badly.

She could tell she had passed some sort of test with him, and that having passed the test, the power had shifted between them. That night at the hotel, she was aware of him staring at her as she opened her door. The stare was electric. She had only recently accepted that her desire had less to do with whom she was attracted to, and everything to do with whom she wanted to attract.

She played her hand riskily, bet the house. She walked into his room while he was transcribing his notes, unbuttoned her blouse. He took over from there, for which she was thankful.

She didn't—doesn't—consider herself especially attractive. She makes a handsome first impression—a fit figure, a wedge of auburn hair, a long neck—but on second look, her left eyelid droops slightly, and the asymmetry cancels out her best feature, her wild eyebrows, which she grooms weekly. Just before she met her husband, the lid miraculously found its way open, lending her face an astonished look, and, unbeknownst to her, she became extremely beautiful. The lid sank again a year later, but by then she had already met her husband. More important, she had been given a tease of the charmed life she might have lived had her left eyelid been two millimeters higher.

The first time her husband introduced her to his mother, eighty-seven years old and living in a Jewish retirement home in Buffalo, the old woman took one glance at C-2, at the apex of her beauty, then looked at her middle-aged son and asked a question that C-2, at twenty-four, hadn't yet thought to ask herself: Who is going to take care of him in his old age?

If C-2 is sequestered, she will only have to take care of herself—a much-needed respite justified by civic duty. If something should happen—the dreaded fall—there is always the alternate to take her place.

The judge is still waiting.

C-2 doesn't raise her hand.

. . .

The jury box is now full, five women including C-2, and two men, F-17 and the twitchy alternate with the hectic buzz cut who doesn't pay attention when the judge explains what a *voir dire* is. The alternate is too busy admiring the defense counsel, the woman in her early thirties with the disruptively full figure. C-2 notes a shimmer when the young woman crosses her legs under the table. She is wearing nylons in August in Central Florida.

To C-2's left, the woman in her mid-sixties who had identified herself as a homemaker and member of the First Calvary Baptist congregation raises her hand. "Where's our other half?" she asks the judge. "Aren't there supposed to be twelve of us?"

"Florida only requires a six-person jury in all but capital cases," the judge explains.

The prosecutor, rotund, places both hands flat on the table and jacks himself up. He struggles to button his suit, gives up, and then flashes the jury an aw-shucks grin to let them know he is a local boy, not someone hired from South Florida. He rifles through the questionnaires the jury had filled out earlier that day, with all their stats—profession, married or single, children, felonies—and asks if anyone has concerns about being able to wait until they've heard all the evidence before making up their minds.

C-2 has never had the patience to listen to someone else's story and not try to guess the ending. But guessing the ending is different than calcifying into certitude. She would be willing to switch sides if persuaded, but that wouldn't stop her from speculating. Who honestly imagines themselves to be that neutral and fair?

She glances around at the other potential jurors. They are all nodding affirmatively, certain of their neutrality and fairness, except F-17.

He raises his hand. "Isn't the belief that you won't rush to judgment proof that you will?" he says.

C-2 can see that he hopes his syllogism will get him dismissed.

But the prosecutor looks away, as if a new idea has just occurred to him. "Do you read the newspaper?" he asks the woman seated directly in front of C-2. The chairs in the back row sit on a riser. C-2 can see the woman's scalp through her cornrows. The woman is white and the stalks blond. The ruts in between are sunburned.

"H-8," the woman says. "I use the newspaper for my parrot's droppings."

"Let's talk about doubt," the prosecutor says. "Reasonable doubt versus an abiding conviction of doubt."

The church lady raises her hand. "What does 'abiding' mean?"

"The court isn't allowed to define terms," the judge intervenes. "And you can't look up the word on your smartphone tonight. You aren't allowed to consider any information, including the definition of a word, outside this court. I dismissed a juror last year for looking up 'prudent.'"

The prosecutor studies his polished shoes until the judge finishes. "Let's talk about common sense," he says, walking over to the church lady. "How did you decide what to eat for breakfast?"

"I looked in my fridge."

"So you accepted the evidence before you and made a decision."

"I had scrambled eggs."

"Okay, let's take a more important decision, one that you had to think hard about." He looks over at F-17. "Are you married?"

"No," F-17 says.

"You?" the prosecutor asks C-2.

"Yes."

"How did you decide to marry your husband?"

"Our accountant told us we would save money on taxes," she says.

They'd been living together for over five years. They loved each other. The money could be spent on a vacation, something they had never allowed themselves. They had traveled extensively on assignment, but only to places where the tourists had fled. This time they decided to go somewhere exotic where there wasn't a war. But without a war, they almost killed each other.

"So you would say your decision making is more swayed by facts than emotion?" asks the prosecutor.

"Yes," C-2 says.

A hand goes up, the twitchy alternate's. "Why are you asking us all these questions? Why don't they have professional jurors?"

· · ·

The defense counsel's *voir dire* is calculated to give her a catbird seat.

"Have you heard of Stockholm syndrome?" she asks the jury. To those jurors who don't nod yes, she explains, "Stockholm syndrome is a psychological term used to describe the paradoxical bond that develops between a captor and a hostage.

"Do you believe such a bond can exist?" she asks A-9, the chemical engineer and only African American on the jury.

"Yes."

"What if it isn't a literal captor and hostage? What if the captor and hostage are family members?" she asks F-17.

"Which family members?" he asks right back.

"Sisters."

He thinks before he answers, "Yes."

"Twins?" she asks B-7, the middle school teacher dressed for an after-hours club.

"Yes."

The jury consultant signals the defense counsel back to the desk to confer. While they strategize, C-2 notices the defendant sneak a piece of chocolate from an open candy-bar wrapper on her lap.

The defense counsel returns to the jury box, walking the length of its wooden rail. "Do you personally know someone who would fall somewhere on the autism spectrum?" she asks no one in particular. "Family members?"

The church lady and the blonde with cornrows raise their hands.

The defense counsel glances over at her jury expert, who doesn't seem concerned about the familial knowledge of those who lack emotional intelligence.

"Do you believe that innocent people are capable of false confessions?" she asks the church lady.

The church lady looks skeptical.

"What if that person is autistic and lacks the capacity to distinguish between falsehood and truth?"

"I guess" is her answer.

The defense counsel's final question is for C-2: "Can you be objective about the death of a child and give it no more or less weight than the death of an adult?"

C-2 watches the defendant twist a shank of her harlequin hair. Is the pattern a calculated distraction or did they take away her black shoe polish when they arrested her and those are her natural roots? Markings always serve a purpose. The zebra's stripes keep away the flies.

When C-2 had tired of photographing the human species, she started photographing animals—the work she is best known for. Her most reprinted series is about mothers trying to protect their young from predators. But rather than photograph the battle and kill, C-2 shot close-ups of the mother's face at the moment she realized that her calf or fledgling or cub was doomed. Some of the mothers looked stricken, others hysterical.

For each expression she managed to capture, C-2 suffered weeks of bereavement. You don't accidentally stumble across scenes like that: You track the mothers and infants for weeks. You get to know them as individuals. People think they understand what a kill is like because they've streamed a YouTube clip of a lion attacking a baby elephant. But a kill smells. You can hear chewing. Bones snapping doesn't sound at all like wood cracking. And then there are the howls and caws and bellowing of the mothers.

C-2's gaze moves to the middle-aged woman seated in the gallery, but she and the defendant's prettier version have fled. The defendant also notices her family's defection. She turns around in her chair, and C-2 can see her face again. On second look, the defendant's face isn't anything like a symmetrical how-to-draw face. One side of her lip is pulled up. Contempt? The only asymmetrical expression.

The defense counsel is waiting for C-2 to answer. She repeats, "Can you be objective about the death of a child?"

"Yes," C-2 says.

. . .

The potential jury, seven of them including the alternate, wait in the hall while the lawyers horse-trade.

The blonde with the cornrows says to anyone one who will listen, "What's with the defendant's hair?"

"Did you notice the twin?" asks the church lady.

"We're not allowed to discuss the case," says the schoolteacher.

C-2 walks over to F-17. She has always wanted to photograph a dissection, a contemporary cross between Rembrandt's *The Anatomy Lesson* and Vesalius's anatomical illustrations.

"If one of us gets tossed," she says to him, "can I get your number and email?"

Before C-2 can finish her question, she realizes that F-17 thinks she is trying to pick him up. He looks surprised, but intrigued.

"I'm a photographer," she explains. "Would it be possible for me to attend your class and photograph a dissection?"

The bailiff calls them back into the courtroom before F-17 can answer.

"The trial begins Monday morning at nine a.m. sharp," the judge says after the six of them, and the alternate, are sworn in. "You are not allowed to Google or watch or stream or upload or read anything about this case. You are not allowed to discuss this case with anyone, including spouses and best friends who promise they won't say anything. You took an oath."

She reminds the jury to pack any medications they need in case of sequestration.

C-2 can't help but wonder which meds her fellow jurors are on.

.   .   .

The afternoon squall has already begun by the time the judge dismisses them. The jurors huddle under the courthouse's overhang, waiting for the downpour to let up. They have just learned too much about one another—what they ate for breakfast, how they decided to marry, if they jump to conclusions—and now they must press together to keep dry.

The first one to brave a drenching is H-8, Cornrows. She takes off her flip-flops and makes a barefoot dash for the SUV parked selfishly over the white line. The twitchy alternate goes next. He accepts that he is going to get wet and strolls off to the bus stop. The church lady has come prepared with an umbrella. She offers to share it. The chemical engineer and the schoolteacher take her up on the offer and they slosh together to their cars.

The rain is relentless, the overhang a waterfall, the steps rapids, the parking lot a floodplain.

F-17 and C-2 are the only ones left. Has he waited so that he can be alone with her? Does he think she has waited so that she can be alone with him? She regrets the miscommunication earlier, and then she doesn't regret it.

"You would need to get permission from the families," he says, as if nothing had transpired between their last conversation and now.

"Of course I would speak to the families first," she says. "I wouldn't photograph faces, or anything else that could identify them. I'm only interested in what's under the skin."

"Everyone looks as different inside as they do outside."

"No two spleens look alike?"

"Some people have three spleens. Some people have two pancreases. One in seven is lacking a palmaris muscle." He points to the muscle on his forearm, the ridge from his wrist to his elbow.

"But the heart is always on the left side," C-2 says.

"Not necessarily. People with dextrocardia have a mirror heart on their right side," F-17 says. "Let me think about it. These are my patients."

The cloudburst is over.

"We remove the faces first. Maybe once that's done," he says.

Did you get out of jury duty?" her husband says as soon as she walks in the door. Her husband has been home alone all day, writing his memoir—this despite the fact that when he was at the apex of his career, he said that he pitied old war correspondents who wrote their memoirs. "Did Jimmy's 'In God We Trust' craziness work?" he asks before she can take off her wet shoes.

They live at the end of a dirt road on a private lake. The house is midcentury, 80 percent glass. It took them weeks to scrape off the gluey residual of taped *X*s after the last hurricane blew through. They agreed that they would rather chance being decapitated by flying glass than tape the windows ever again.

She tells him she is on a murder trial.

"First-degree?" he asks.

"You know I can't discuss it."

She starts dinner, a simple salad. Neither of them cooks, though they own a six-burner stove. When he comes out of his study half an hour later, she knows he knows more about the case than she does.

"I wish you hadn't done that," she says. "It's hard enough for me to stay away from my computer."

"What harm is there if I know?"

"Because now every time I look at you, I know you are keeping a secret from me."

"It's not a secret. It's all over the internet."

"Who did she kill?" C-2 asks.

"Who is she *accused* of killing," her husband corrects her.

"I'm going to find out Monday anyway."

He doesn't answer her.

She says, "This is exactly why you shouldn't have done it. You're ruining our last weekend together."

His poker face softens into bafflement. He is—and has always been—a handsome man, if slightly abbreviated in the legs: flinty profile, white hair thick enough to cantilever over his brow.

"I may be sequestered," she says.

She can see by his reaction that whatever was all over the internet heralds a protracted trial.

"For how long?" he asks.

"The judge told us to pack enough medicine for three weeks."

She watches his face as he tries to process what her absence will mean. Being alone for twenty-one days at eighty-six, cocooned in your diminishing senses—this is a different level of loneliness than she has ever experienced.

"Should we get someone to stay with you?" she asks.

He has a stepson by a former wife only two hours away, friends, neighbors, but he will have no one beside him at night if he should wake up light-headed and unable to orient himself in the dark, or feel his heart fluttering, or his legs cramping.

Her husband is—and has always been—a hypochondriac, but recently, he has finally outgrown his disorder. All the imaginary symptoms are coming true.

"I'm not an invalid," he says.

"We could have Jimmy come by once a day."

"I don't want Jimmy watching TV in the living room while I'm trying to write."

"Do you want me to ask the judge to dismiss me? There's an alternate."

She can see how much he wants to say yes.

"That's ridiculous," he says, and finishes his salad. The second he puts down his fork, he asks, "Will I be able to reach you?"

"Of course. I think."

. . .

He loads the dishwasher, while C-2 retreats to her studio, a barn-size addition off the garage, sparsely furnished and clean as an operating theater. She spends the evening leafing through art books, searching for paintings of dissections, a surprisingly popular subject matter over the centuries. Every medical school and surgeon's guild commissioned one. Rembrandt's first painting after he had arrived in Amsterdam, twenty-five and ambitious, was *The Anatomy Lesson of Dr. Tulp*. His genius was to compose Dr. Tulp and his medical students and the cadaver as a single shape, splintered by light and dark, the first group portrait in which individualism melded into the collective. The cadaver was a common thief, the body purchased after his hanging. Dr. Tulp is tugging on what C-2 suspects is the palmaris muscle, the muscle that controlled the fingers that stole.

"What are you so absorbed in?" her husband asks, leaning in the doorway.

She shows him the illustration in the book and tells him about F-17, the anatomy professor who is on the jury with her. "He said if I got the family's permission, I could photograph a dissection."

"You told me you wanted your next series to be more life affirming," he says.

"I would never use the words 'life affirming.'"

"Lighter. That was the word you used."

"I said I never wanted to photograph another kill."

"So instead you want to photograph a dissection?"

"It's completely different. It's the opposite of a kill."

"But you didn't photograph the kill. You photographed the mother's face. Somebody somewhere is grieving for those cadavers."

He comes up behind her and kisses her neck, his prelude to intimacy.

She has just spent the past hour looking at dissections. She is hardly in the mood.

"I'm going to miss you so much," he says, rubbing her shoulders. His nails have aged faster than anything else on his person, the keratin less lacquer than hoof. When he massages her shoulders, as he is doing now, the hardened nails sometimes spoil his gentle touch.

All happy families are happy in the same way; all unhappy families are unhappy in their own way. She would add to Tolstoy's dictum: All happy marriages have sex; all unhappy marriages don't.

They still have sex, but nothing she would have called, at sixteen, "all the way." He doesn't so much possess her as haunt her. At the best of times, she can still marvel at how intrepidly he wants sex. Potency, technique, performance have been replaced by something more basic—the will to live while alive. His height and mass may have lessened with age, but his life force has only grown denser and more combustible. Their lovemaking doesn't pivot on potency and technique; it does something far more intimate and abiding.

It slays C-2.

Monday morning her husband drives her to court in case of sequestration—they share the Prius. Their other vehicle, a rusty beater they had driven down from New York City twelve years ago, has sprouted lichen after an especially rainy summer and then sunk into the gum-mud by the lake, a hairy mammoth caught in a tar pit.

The courthouse is a four-story utilitarian marble cube in a sun-struck plaza, more Soviet than Le Corbusier. The town is the county seat, the biggest employer a land-grant university. Her husband had taken an endowed professorship at the journalism college after retiring from the *Times* but resigned after only two semesters. He told C-2 that he didn't want to give away to youth all the tricks it had taken him a lifetime to figure out for himself. But C-2 knew the real reason: he was worried he would become a blowhard and talk away his memoir before he wrote it. They stayed because C-2 had started photographing her *Mother* series, and the lake by the house provided a scaly menagerie of predators.

As C-2 and her husband drive by the courthouse, television reporters and crews mill around the entrance, vying for the meager shade of three date palms. Armed with satellite dishes, a convoy of news vans block the curb, and a bus from the Villages—a megalopolis-size retirement community sixty miles south—idles across the street.

"I'm going to be sequestered, aren't I?" C-2 says.

"How would I know?" her husband asks.

"You went online. Who did she kill?"

"She's accused of killing her eighteen-month-old brother."

"How?"

"Setting him on fire."

Her husband steers them into the courthouse's underground garage, a maze of deep contrasts after such a sunny morning. He parks outside the jury entrance and gets out of the car, walking toward her with the caution of someone who can hardly find his way in the dim light. They embrace. He has lost three inches over the years and she is now taller than he is. Whenever her chin rests on his head, she feels more protective than passionate.

"I may not see you for three weeks," he says. "I love you so much."

He kisses her, open-mouthed. He wants to make this a lover's parting, but C-2 can feel his anxiety about returning to the empty house.

She whispers, "I'll ask for conjugal visits."

. . .

Inside the building, after her overnight bag with its provisions of pills is searched, and her phone and tablet requisitioned and bagged, the deputy escorts C-2 to the jury lounge, a classroom-size window-less hold filled with dentist waiting room furniture and old issues of *AARP* and *Entertainment Weekly.*

As she enters the room, F-17 looks up from his book, a sci-fi paperback fat enough to last three weeks. He shares the sofa with the chemical engineer, who is eating a power bar, and the alternate, who is reading a greyhound racing tip sheet. Everyone has brought an overnight bag.

"Are we being sequestered?" C-2 asks.

"No one has told us anything," F-17 says.

"You saw the news trucks," the alternate says.

"I understand the media frenzy over George Zimmerman or the loud-music murderer, but why a teenage girl?" the schoolteacher asks.

"She's rich and she's white," the chemical engineer says.

"Quiet," the deputy chides.

Cornrows arrives next, hauling an extra-large suitcase, as if she were going on a cruise.

"I brought a bathing suit," she announces to no one in particular. "My boyfriend's sister cleans at the Econo Lodge off I-75 and she says that's where they'll put us. It has a pool."

. . .

The deputy lines them up, the six jurors and the alternate, according to their assigned seats, and they file through the door.

Even festooned with flags and gold seals, the courtroom is nondescript, with beige walls and an acoustic-board ceiling. The chairs look like they were purchased in bulk from an online catalog, the court reporter is a blowsy blonde chewing gum, the judge has a sixteen-ounce Jamba Juice by her gavel, yet C-2 is humbled. She doesn't consider herself a judgmental person, though judge she does—all the time. She judges her friend and colleague who got a MacArthur grant for her random, blurry snapshots; she judges her mother for choosing cruel boyfriends; she judges photography contests where she'd rather go blind than give an honorable mention to the tasteless photo of a homeless person. But this judgment is something else entirely. This judgment is as close as mortals get to God. She can sense that the other jurors are humbled as well. Even Cornrows, wearing her flip-flops, comports herself with dignity.

The gallery is packed with press and seniors. C-2 had read somewhere that the Villages bus their citizens all over Central Florida to attend celebrity trials, a pastime more engrossing than shuffleboard.

"Good morning," the judge says to the jury after they take their seats. "I am sequestering you. I am also ruling that your identities will remain undisclosed during the trial. Attorneys will refer to you only by your letter and number, not name. In addition, I am warning the media not to photograph you. Anyone"—she looks out at the gallery—"including the public caught publishing or posting photos of the jurors on Instagram or Facebook will be held in contempt of court. You will do jail time, ladies and gentlemen."

She waits for the bailiff to hand out notebooks and pencils to the jury.

"You are allowed to takes notes for your own use," the judge instructs them, "but don't get so distracted taking notes that you don't pay attention to other clues. Notes are not a substitute for memory. Transcripts are not a substitute for memory. It's not only what a witness says, it is also whether or not you believe them."

Only C-2, F-17, and the twitchy alternate open their notebooks. The rest leave them on their laps or put them under their chairs.

The judge reads the charges—one count of second-degree murder and three counts of first-degree arson—and asks if the state is ready to proceed with opening remarks.

The rotund prosecutor stands, faces the jury, and wishes them a good morning. This time as he tries to button his jacket, the button slips easily into place. On an empty easel that was standing at the ready when the jury walked in, he places a poster-size full-color photograph of a not particularly pretty baby. C-2 catches a glimpse of the back of the photograph. It was printed at OfficeMax.

"Caleb Karl Butler, eighteen months old, didn't die in a fire. Caleb was *set on* fire. How do we know?" He points to the defendant. "Because she told us."

Someone has taken the defendant to the beauty parlor. Her black fringe has been shorn off and the blond strands shaped into an old-fashioned pageboy.

C-2 writes down:

somebody loves her

"Caleb's diaper had been soaked in paint thinner," the prosecutor continues. "Paint thinner isn't a good accelerant. When the arson expert tried to replicate the origin of the fire, it took him nine minutes and forty-three matches to light a similar diaper."

C-2 writes:

defendant blinks 68 xs a minute

"What was Caleb doing as his sister struck match after match and couldn't get his diaper to catch fire? Let yourself imagine." He mimics striking forty-three wooden matches. He takes his full nine minutes, waiting for the imaginary flames to burn out before striking the next one. If C-2 had her camera, she would take a close-up of Caleb's mother's face. She sits in the front row, on the defense side of the aisle, directly behind the defendant, but she won't look in her daughter's direction. If she did, she would only see the back of the newly coiffed pageboy. The prettier sister isn't with her today.

The prosecutor asks permission to show the jury a photograph, but the defense objects. When the judge studies the picture, her civic veneer falters and her eyes widen. She rules the photograph too prejudicial, but the prosecutor has another picture to share, and this time the defense lets it slide.

The chemical engineer, seated in the first chair, is offered the photograph. She stiffens before daring to look, and then quickly hands it to F-17. He examines it thoroughly, jots something in his notebook, and hands it to the church lady. It is apparent that the church lady has no idea what she is looking at—and then she does. She quickly passes it along until it reaches C-2. It's an eight-by-ten of the melted crib.

"After the defendant sets her brother's diaper on fire, she closes the nursery door on what must have been Caleb's screams. He was eighteen months old, for God's sake. She sets two more fires—one in her twin sister's bedroom and one in her own. She calls 911 at 4:38— six minutes after she closes the nursery door—and tells the operator, I quote, 'I think I smell smoke.'" He says this in a falsetto key to imitate a young girl's high register, presumably the defendant's, though C-2 knows the jury may never hear her voice. "'Thinks'? 'Smoke'? She doesn't mention that there is a baby inside the house."

The defense objects to something the prosecutor just said and another sidebar is called.

C-2 is still holding the image of the melted crib. No one has come to retrieve it from her and enter it into evidence. She doesn't know what to do with it. Facedown so she can concentrate on the proceedings, or faceup so she can confront exactly what she is being asked to judge?

.   .   .

At noon sharp, the court recesses for lunch.

Without being told where they will be dining, the jury is ushered into a windowless van. Minutes later, the van parks and the deputy rolls back the door. They are eating at Nic & Gladys Luncheonette, courtesy of the court. C-2 has driven by this place for years and always thought it was abandoned. But there really are a Nic and Gladys, two older West Indians. The jury and the deputy are the only customers this afternoon. The choices are chalked on a board, in pristine handwriting. Fried pork chop or London broil. C-2 is a vegetarian. She asks if she can just order sides, rice and green beans.

Gladys puts on a hairnet to scoop up the sides, while Nic works the deep fryer. When the food comes out, before anyone has had a chance to dig in, the church lady says grace by herself while the twitchy alternate asks the deputy where they will be having dinner tonight.

"Outback Steakhouse."

"We get to order anything we want? Does that include alcohol?" the alternate wants to know.

"The state isn't paying for your drinks," says the deputy.

"Are we allowed a glass of wine with dinner if we pay for it ourselves?" asks the chemical engineer.

"One," says the deputy.

"You're shitting me," says the alternate.

While the jury waits for dessert—a choice between red velvet cake or Neapolitan ice cream—Cornrows turns to the chemical engineer and, indicating her fraying stalks, asks, "How do I wash them? No offense or anything, I just thought you'd know."

"You don't wash them, you soak them in a cup of olive oil overnight," says the chemical engineer. She wears her hair meticulously clipped on the sides with a sculpted plateau overhead. "Don't forget to mix it with a cup of coconut oil. You don't want your hair smelling like a salad."

"How do I keep the oil from dripping on everything?"

The chemical engineer smiles. In profile, she makes a striking Nefertiti. She has no more idea of how to wash cornrows than C-2 does. "Did you bring a bathing cap?"

"Do you want to go outside for a smoke?" F-17 asks C-2.

"Are we allowed?" she asks the deputy—ex-military, by his scars and stance.

He tells her and F-17 to stand just outside the door where he can see them. On the far side of the glass window, C-2 stations herself in the sun. F-17 leans against the faded Nic & Gladys Luncheonette sign, painted decades ago in the same penmanship found on the blackboard.

He offers her a cigarette.

"I don't smoke," she reminds him.

"Neither do I."

He lights her cigarette and then his own. They both hold the burning tips away and downwind. The sun feels kind after the artificial chill of indoor Florida.

"I brought a carton," he says, smiling.

.   .   .

The deputy hands C-2 a note when they return to the jury room. It reads: *Your husband called.*

"He wants to know if you've been sequestered," the deputy says.

"Did you tell him yes? Am I allowed to call him back?"

"You can give me the message and I'll relay it."

We are being sequestered, she writes on a page torn from her notebook. *I will phone you as soon as I am allowed. Call Jimmy if you need anything. Don't be a martyr.*

She crosses out the last line and hands the note to the bailiff.

"We are being sequestered," she hears the bailiff tell her husband. "I will call you as soon as I am allowed. Phone Jimmy if you need anything. Don't be a martyr."

She can't hear her husband's lengthy reply, but she can see the bailiff growing impatient.

"No, you can't talk to her at this time," the bailiff says.

.   .   .

The prosecutor is restless to get started. He doesn't bother to button his jacket. "We know how she did it, now I'm going to tell you why. Jealousy, oldest motive in the world. Caleb was a miracle baby. Mr. Butler was fifty and Mrs. Butler was forty-four when she discovered she was pregnant after a lifetime of trying. Twelve years before, the Butlers had adopted the defendant, Anca, and her twin sister, Stephana, age five, from a *Romanian orphanage.*" The italics are his. He waits a beat for the jurors to construct their own internal visions of a Romanian orphanage—neglected infants in factory-size rooms, the back of their heads flattened from never being picked up.

The defense objects, and another sidebar is called. The prosecutor looks over at the jury and all but rolls his eyes, letting them know that he's got motive galore, if only the defense would shut up.

All afternoon, C-2 takes notes as the prosecutor tells tales about Anca's tantrums and the revolving specialists and the evolving diagnoses, a checklist of all the things that can go wrong in childhood and adolescence—friendless, fat, bullied, and bullying.

C-2's final note of the day:

The prosecution has no idea why she did it

C ornrows's earlier tip proves on the mark—the jury is staying at the Econo Lodge across the interstate from Silver Springs, a lagoon-blue lake braided in jungle vines, where the first *Tarzan* movies were filmed. The Econo Lodge sits on the treeless side of the eight-lane interstate, a two-story stucco building with a fiberglass pool. The hotel's bright orange sign with its whirlpool design and twinkling star is reminiscent of a Tide detergent box.

The jurors are the only guests.

After telling them that breakfast will be served in the lobby at seven a.m., the Indian woman who commandeers the front desk assigns each juror a room, but doesn't hand out key cards.

C-2's assigned room is on the second floor, between the open-air landing with the noisy ice machine and F-17's room. Below her is the church lady, who tells C-2 she is a light sleeper and asks her not to wear shoes when in her room. Cornrows has scored the only one-bedroom suite, which the alternate insinuates is cronyism because her boyfriend's sister cleans here.

The deputy cuts him off. "Your rooms have been prepared according to the court's mandate. You will not be allowed to lock your doors from the inside. The chains and bolts have been removed. The cable and wifi have been disabled, but the TVs have DVD players, and movies are available at the front desk. Questions?"

"Do we get maid service?" asks the church lady.

"When do we leave for Outback?" asks the alternate.

"Must we go?" asks C-2.

She, the chemical engineer, and F-17 opt for takeout.

. . .

The room has two twin beds, a patterned rug to hide stains, one reading lamp, blackout curtains, and a surprisingly clean bathroom. The view is of passing semis. Her husband would never deign to stay in places like this, but when C-2 travels alone, she secretly likes these undistinguished stopovers, though she always packs her own sheets.

She instinctively picks up the remote to test the TV and is met with the promised nothingness.

C-2 has brought two novels for company, though lately she is more inclined to read nonfiction—history, science, biography. She chose novels because she has read that fiction enhances compassion and she suspects she will need all the mercy she can muster for the Romanian orphan. One of the novels is a thick thriller her husband recommended and the other is a new translation of *Madame Bovary*, which she has meant to reread for years.

She kicks off her shoes, stretches out on the bed nearest the air conditioner, and flicks on the reading lamp. A haze of cold LED slopes onto the pillow. She weighs both novels literally, one in each hand, but neither appeals. After hearing the story of the immolation of Caleb, the thriller's hair-raisers will seem too tame, and Madame Bovary's adultery too silly.

She wanders over to the window. In addition to the passing semis, her room looks over the rectangular pool, which is long enough to have a deep end and a shallow end. The pool is set back from the highway, in a grassy area shielded by pines. Four chaise lounges, two occupied by feral cats, share the tiny concrete deck. A cyclone fence tall enough to meet safety regulations and choked in kudzu is the only landscaping.

F-17 has remembered his bathing suit. He is swimming laps, diagonally so as to achieve the longest stretch before he has to turn. C-2 is a swimmer herself, though she didn't think to pack a suit. F-17 does a solid flip against the shallow-end corner and begins his crawl and kick. No unnecessary splashing. She approves of his stroke.

She slips into shorts and crosses the parking lot to the pool. At least she can dip her feet in. Besides, she wants F-17's medical opinion of the defendant's rapid, persistent blinking.

He is reclining on a chaise lounge, eyes shut against the low sun. He hasn't bothered to towel off and the water beads on his chest, the skin startlingly smooth in contrast to his pitted face. He looks younger than forty-two, the age he gave during the *voir dire*. His hair is a black that doesn't cast red in the sun. If he let it grow, he would have ringlets. But he keeps it short enough that each strand only has one chance to complete a circle, the kind of Platonic ideal you find in the ringlets on the marble bust of a Roman general.

Her shadow causes him to open his eyes.

"May I ask you something?" she says. She does not recline on the adjacent chaise, but sits on its unstable edge. "What causes rapid eye blinking?"

"How rapid?" he asks.

"Sixty-eight times a minute."

"Are you asking me as an anatomist or as a juror?"

"It's a medical question."

"Rapid blinking blocks vision. You basically close your eyelids so there's less information coming into the brain."

"I read somewhere it was a sign of lying," she says.

"Actually, people blink more when they daydream than when they lie."

. . .

It is still bright and sunny at seven when her takeout arrives—an Outback salad and a baked potato. She eats in her room, on the spare bed. There is no chair. One Styrofoam container is hot, the other cold. She opens the baked potato first so she can eat it while it still holds an atom of heat. Then she rips open the clear bag containing the plastic utensils and one stingy napkin. Concentrating on each forkful, she slowly chews the potato's flesh. Whenever she eats alone these days, she uses the opportunity to practice eating alone after her husband is dead, when she will be eating alone for real. His mother lived to ninety-six, but that doesn't mean he will.

C-2 has come to accept that the last ten years of a life are as transformative as the first ten. But how do you know when the countdown begins? Her husband has always emitted excess heat, now he is constantly cold. Is that number ten of the countdown? Or did the countdown begin last year when he had the pacemaker put in?

Her potato is cold.

She wants out of this motel room.

Now.

She heads to the lobby to pick out one of the approved DVDs for the evening. F-17 is already there, choosing among three approved VHS cassettes. He holds them up for her opinion—*Teenage Mutant Ninja Turtles, Dora the Explorer,* and *Amadeus,* the story of Salieri, a mediocre court composer, and his murderous envy of Mozart. C-2 saw both the play and the movie. The promise of Mozart's music is irresistible.

"Are we allowed to watch a movie together?" she asks the night deputy, a fully made-up state-fair beauty queen with a badge.

"Sorry. You can't be alone together, and I have to stay here," she says in an unexpectedly husky voice.

F-17 offers C-2 the videocassette.

"My room only has a DVD player," she says.

.   .   .

Once again, C-2 stretches out on the twin bed nearest the air conditioner and listens to Mozart through the gypsum wall, which masks
nothing. She can practically distinguish the instruments. When
the music stops and the muffled dialogue begins, she goes outside
into the humid night air. The outdoor walkway that connects the
second-story rooms smells faintly of ammonia and mold. Next to
the open stairwell, under a cold spotlight, in a funnel of moths, the
ice machine hums. She leans against the iron railing. She can see
the front office from here. The deputy is gone. She doesn't appear to
be in the parking lot, either. The music starts up again, *The Magic
Flute*. She knocks on F-17's door. He is barefoot in an unbuttoned
shirt and jeans. He doesn't seem all that surprised to see her.

His room has a queen-size bed.

"May I come in?" she asks.

"We could be thrown off the jury," he says, closing the door
behind her.

"I need music," she says.

"Do you want me to start the movie over?"

"No," she says.

There is no chair in his room, either. She sits on the edge of the
mattress.

"You comfortable?" he asks, lying down.

"Fine," she says.

"Here. I'll sit up and you can lie down," he says.

"I'm being ridiculous." She reclines beside him. Then, to her
surprise, she adds, "It's not like we can lock the door."

.   .   .

C-2 can't concentrate on Salieri's jealousy of Mozart any more than she could on Jack Reacher's fisticuffs or Emma Bovary's vexation at the way her husband slurps soup.

She didn't come to F-17's room for the music alone. She is curious to see if their flirtation can withstand the harrowing stories they were told this afternoon. A flirtation would make the sequestered nights more interesting.

His hands are folded behind his head—she can see his palmaris muscle. His ankles are crossed. He has beautiful feet.

She would like one last dalliance before she gets too old. She's done the math. If her husband lives another ten years, his mother's life-span, she will be sixty-two—young for a widow, but old for a dalliance.

She is fairly certain that he isn't watching the movie either. But fairly isn't certain. What if she is delusional—or, worse, pathetic?

She closes her eyes. There is only music now, and a palpable awareness of his body next to hers. *Don Giovanni* is playing. The saddest opera, and the saddest song in the saddest opera is sung by Death.

She rolls over and kisses him.

After a surprised hesitation, he kisses her back. His kiss is lengthy, compelling, carnal and ethereal at once, and she is ashamed of how badly she needed it.

She pulls back, slowly, and opens her eyes. The lights are on. The bedspread is orange and purple. The walls have heel marks. The ceiling is cottage cheese. A band of static cuts across Salieri's face on the screen. She is once again a fifty-two-year-old woman watching a movie with a fellow juror at an Econo Lodge.

"I'm sorry, this is a mistake," she says, but she knows she doesn't sound sorry. She sounds flirtatious, which isn't her intention. The heady aftermath of the kiss has changed her voice into something she doesn't recognize.

"Sorry for what?" he asks.

"You need to ask?"

"We are two private citizens doing public service. Our nights are our own."

"Unless we invite the deputy in to observe us, our nights are not our own," she says.

He holds her wrist before she can get up, then lets go.

"Thank you," he says.

"What for?" she says.

"You need to ask?"

He goes downstairs to return the video and distract the deputy, while she slips back into her room. It's still twilight, not yet nine o'clock. She brought a three weeks' supply of Ambien, as per the judge's instructions. She takes one.

Supine, eyes shut, knowing drugged sleep will soon arrive, she allows herself to remember the kiss, but the music, which is playing jarringly loud inside her skull, keeps distracting. *Don Giovanni.*

The first time she heard the opera was in middle school. Miss Foxx, her music appreciation teacher, had assigned the class to listen to the classical radio station that evening and take notes about how the music made them feel. "Try for the sublime," Miss Foxx had instructed C-2 and her eleven-year-old classmates, the sons and daughters of casino workers, for whom the only sublime was a jackpot. In Las Vegas, where C-2 lived with her mother in a subdivision with more sand than grass, the assignment was as close to a field trip as the school provided.

C-2 and her mother had owned a cassette player and a TV, but not a radio, except in the car. After dinner, C-2 sat in the garage behind the wheel of her mother's VW Beetle, and tuned the radio to the local classical station. Her mother had started the engine and left the car in park so that C-2 wouldn't run down the battery.

At first C-2 felt stupid writing down her feelings about classical music. Without a snappy beat, the music seemed pointless.

On the far side of the Beetle's windshield, she could see her secondhand bike with its flat tire that her mother never got around to fixing, and the paint cans left over from the time she and her mother had painted her bedroom purple, a favorite color C-2 soon came to hate, and the empty pizza box from dinner sticking out of the trash can. She shut her eyes against all this ugliness, and without warning, there was only music. Blind, she was no longer bored by the music. It made her want to cry.

The garage door opened and her mother had come charging toward her, screaming her name. "What was I thinking?" she told C-2. "You could have died from the fumes."

C-2 has always wondered if what she experienced in that garage— the sublime, as Miss Foxx named it—resulted from the music or the carbon monoxide. But what stayed with her, what shaped her nature, was that she now knew that the sublime existed and she was just as entitled to it as the girls who had radios in their pretty bedrooms.

It was only a kiss.

F-17 is already at the breakfast table, a folding affair with benches, when C-2 walks into the improvised buffet off the lobby. The church lady is chewing off his ear. As C-2 approaches, his steady amused stare is meant to convey that he has been waiting for her.

"Can I bum a cigarette?" she asks him.

"We're going outside for a smoke," he tells the deputy, the ex-military from yesterday.

They walk over to a shaded picnic table near the pool, still within the deputy's crosshairs. This time when F-17 lights her cigarette, she doesn't hold it downwind. She inhales.

"I've been thinking about you all night," he says.

"I took an Ambien," she says.

"I should have been thinking about the trial."

"It was only a kiss. We're adults," she says, but she doesn't sound like an adult. She takes a second drag. "I forgot how much I miss smoking."

"You asked me yesterday what causes rapid eye blinking? The longer I observed the defendant, the more convinced I became that she might have blepharospasm, or tardive dyskinesia, the result of all her antipsychotic medications. Blinking is a side effect."

"Or maybe she's just daydreaming," C-2 says, exhaling.

. . .

When C-2 and the other jurors take their chairs, the judge bangs her gavel impatiently for the press and the seniors, occupying the back four pews, to be quiet. She threatens exile to anyone who disrupts the proceedings again, then asks if the defense is ready to present opening remarks.

The defense counsel lays a comforting hand on both of the defendant's shoulders before approaching the jury. Wearing a dark suit with ample room for her full figure, she has her own poster-size photograph to share with the jury—the defendant cradling her little brother Caleb in her arms. Her hair is all black in the picture, shoulder length, bangs that hang past her eyebrows. She looks stiff, but then again, whenever C-2 has been handed an infant by a new mother, she, too, has stiffened. C-2 is childless by choice.

"Anca Butler loved her brother Caleb," the defense counsel says.

Back at the defense table, her client blinks and blinks and blinks.

"Anca didn't start the fires. She was in the backyard feeding the family dogs when the fires started. The instant she smelled smoke, she dialed 911. 'I think I smell smoke,' Anca told the emergency operator."

The defense counsel doesn't quote Anca in a falsetto as the prosecutor did. Instead she speaks the words—"I think I smell smoke"—in the tone of a concerned citizen doing the right thing.

"Only after the 911 operator assured Anca that fire trucks were on their way did Anca see flames in the nursery window. She dropped the phone and ran back into the house to save Caleb, but the fire was everywhere, the heat scorching. You'll hear the prosecutor talk about Anca's singed eyelashes as proof that she set the fires. It is the only physical evidence the prosecutor has. But what he won't tell you is that Anca's long hair wasn't singed, her bangs weren't singed, her eyebrows weren't singed. To understand the significance of her eyelashes being singed while her eyebrows and hair remained untouched, you'll hear from experts about the dynamics of combustion. Intense heat is capable of singeing off eyelashes while leaving eyebrows unaffected. Anca Butler was *never* close enough to the fire—let alone close enough to *set* the fire—to singe her eyebrows and hair.

"When Anca realized she couldn't reach Caleb, she ran into the street to see if the fire trucks were coming. Her sister Stephana's boyfriend's truck was in the driveway, door open, radio playing. A minute later, Tim Rush burst out of the Butlers' front door, coughing, crazed, and screaming at Anca, 'What have you done?'

"He told the firemen, local volunteers who went to high school with him, that he had grabbed his fire extinguisher from his truck bed and tried to save Caleb, but it was too late. Caleb was dead. He told the police that Anca had been the only person home with Caleb when the fires started. Did the police test Tim's hands for traces of accelerant? Did they test his clothes? He was on the scene seconds after the fire started. No, the police took Tim at his word. The police were also locals who had known Tim all his life."

So far, C-2 has only jotted down:

singed eyelashes

She can't stop thinking about the kiss, her bravery and his surprised reaction, and then his thorough and captivating response. She glances over at F-17. He isn't taking notes either.

"So if Anca is innocent, why did she confess?" the defense counsel asks. "You'll hear from experts about a condition called subordinate-dominance disorder—one twin controls the other. In boys, the disorder typically involves physical abuse, but in twin girls, the abuse is psychological. Anca and Stephana were five years old when the Butlers brought them home from Romania. Anca's muteness didn't concern the Butlers at first. They thought that she wasn't mastering English as fast as Stephana, and that's why Stephana did all the talking for them both. To help her to speak, the Butlers tried every kind of speech therapy imaginable. When none worked, they turned to psychiatry."

To force herself to concentrate on the defense counsel's words, C-2 writes down the list of psychotropic medications Anca has taken over the past ten years—*lithium, Tegretol, Divalproex, Lamictal, Depacon, Abilify, Seroquel, Risperdal, Prozac*—even though the judge warned the jury not to take obsessive notes instead of paying attention to nuance.

Below C-2, two chairs to her right, she has an unobstructed view of F-17's open notebook. The page is still empty, his pencil hand still.

"Why did Anca confess to a crime she didn't commit?" asks the defense counsel, then answers before the jury has a chance to fathom why the blinking teenager might tell a fib that would cost her her life. "Because Anca's twin, Stephana, the dominant partner in their private pathology, ordered the confession.

"At ten past five, minutes after the firemen had put out the flames, Stephana arrived home from her afterschool job at Popeyes. Tim told her that Caleb was dead and Anca was the only one home. Did Stephana cry? Did she scream? Did she even ask how the fire happened? No. She ran to the backyard to find her sister.

"Anca had taken refuge in the kennel with her beloved dogs. She was in shock, at her most vulnerable. She had no idea how the fire started, but she had already convinced herself that it was somehow her fault. Stephana was alone with Anca for twenty-two minutes—

long enough to convince Anca that she was not only negligent, but culpable."

C-2 looks over at F-17's notebook. His pencil hand has finally begun to write. In large block letters, he prints:

SMOKE?

Is it a note about the case? Or is it a note to her?
He adds, *BEFORE LUNCH.*

. . .

They stand outside Nic & Gladys, smoking. He too has started inhaling.

"I can't stop thinking about you," he says, but this time when he says it his tone isn't playful and sexy. His voice is deep and raspy with shame. "A young woman's life is at stake."

"I'm so sorry I started this," she says. She is deeply repentant, but she can't allow her face to express the guilt she feels. The deputy is watching through the window.

"You didn't start it," he says.

"It doesn't matter who started it, we have to stop it," she says.

"Agreed," he says.

Their cigarettes burn down to the filters. The deputy tilts back in his chair to reach over and rap on the glass. Nic and Gladys are already serving.

At the communal table, she sits between Cornrows and the chemical engineer. F-17 takes the chair beside the deputy.

Before C-2 can remember what she ordered, Cornrows brings her and F-17 up to speed. "We're not going back to court," she says. "The witness couldn't get here, so we get to go to a movie. We're taking a vote. You want to see *Magic Mike* or *Furious 7*?"

"Can we opt out?" F-17 asks the deputy.

"How many don't want to go to the movies?"

Only C-2, F-17, and the chemical engineer raise their hands.

. . .

In the van back to the motel, he sits next to her in the middle row. They do not speak.

Back in her room, she stretches out on one of the beds and opens the thriller. She skims, reads the first paragraph over again, absorbs nothing. She goes to the window to see if F-17 is swimming.

He does a strong backstroke, confident he will know the wall is there before he touches it, the sign of a competitive swimmer. His final wind-down consists of a slow breaststroke. Hoisting himself out of the deep end, he stands dripping on the concrete deck. He lets the sun dry him, only toweling off his black hair. He steps into his sandals with his beautiful feet and walks over to a chaise lounge facing C-2's room. As he sits, he spies her in the window.

Should she coyly step backward into the shadows and pretend she didn't see him? Why? She will only return to the window a second later to see if he is still looking.

She stares directly at him, and waits for him to look away, but he doesn't.

The van honks for the movie crowd. The two deputies, ex-military and beauty queen, wrangle about who will go and who will stay behind to guard the party poopers. The beauty queen wins and the van takes off.

Even though C-2 and F-17 are separated by fifty feet, and window glass, she marvels at how easily they can agree on a plan.

She has the better vantage point. She will give the signal as soon as she is certain the ex-military isn't watching. The signal is closing the drapes.

While she waits for F-17, she considers undressing and climbing into bed, not even pretending to have the talk about responsibility and citizenship. She is now convinced that the best thing for justice will be for them to have sex. At the very least, they will be able to concentrate again.

But waiting naked in bed implies that the choice is entirely hers. She decides to take a shower instead. He can join her or not.

She hears the door to her room close, the door to the bathroom open. Finally, he slides open the shower door, steps naked into the tub with her, and kisses the back of her neck. She is facing the fiberglass wall, under the showerhead. He turns her around. He already has an erection. Will he fuck her standing up in the tub? How is it even possible? The fiberglass is too slippery despite the nonslip treads. But the longer his kiss lasts, the less the logistics matter. He turns off the water, dries her with a towel, each of her limbs, her breasts. His erection never falters. That sort of male confidence is better than fucking standing up in the shower. He takes her wrist and leads her to bed. She is grateful she had the foresight to turn off the lights and close the blackout curtains. He chooses the twin bed she doesn't sleep on, the one she uses as a dining table, and that only makes his entering her sexier.

C-2 has had affairs before, one-, two-, three-night stands, more to test her moxie and attractiveness than to sate a desire. In truth, she has always preferred her husband to the boys and colleagues with whom she has had assignations on assignment, but lately she hasn't gone on assignment. Lately, she and her husband have been alone by the lake trying to determine if the bruise on his hip is new.

In the void of abandon, she shirks off the habit of caution. She can bite F-17 or buck or squeeze him as tightly as she dares, and she doesn't have to worry about bruising him.

.   .   .

Outside, on the walkway connecting the second-story rooms, C-2 hears the other jurors returning. F-17's penis is still inside her, but the act is over for both of them.

Without exchanging a word, they reach for their clothes. He slips on his wet bathing suit while she peeks out the crevasse of light between the blackout curtains.

"His brother was in a coma," C-2 hears the alternate's insistent voice say as he passes in front of the crack, blotting out the sun. "That's why he killed the guy's family."

"His head is too small for his thick neck, he looks like one of those Zika babies," says Cornrows. "Why would *People* magazine think he's the sexiest man alive?"

A minute passes without another word or footfall. C-2 finishes buttoning her blouse, then steps outside as if for a breath of fresh air, while F-17 waits for the all-clear signal. The signal is a sharp tap on the door.

"What you been up to?" asks Cornrows. She is standing in the twilight less than three feet away. "You missed nothing but pinheads and car chases."

C-2 can't rally an answer.

"I guess you didn't hear yet. We get to Skype with our families after dinner, so we voted to eat takeout Chinese here."

As Cornrows heads off to her room, C-2 turns to signal F-17, but his door is already closing behind him.

. . .

An elderly stranger's face fills the screen when it is C-2's turn to Skype. Only when the frowning lips smile does she recognize her husband.

A deputy sits within hearing distance, in case C-2 is tempted to bring up the trial.

"I've missed you so much," her husband says, unaware that their conversation is being monitored.

"Me, too," she says. She means it. The face is becoming more familiar the longer she looks at it.

"You doing okay?" he asks. "You need anything else?"

"A bathing suit."

"How is the hotel?"

"The sheets are made of cheesecloth."

"I'll buy you a set of sheets from that Beyond place and bring them Saturday. Maybe we can test them out. I hope you asked for conjugal visits."

C-2 can see her own expression in a corner of the screen. She is blinking almost as much as Anca, though her left eyelid, always weaker, takes a beat longer to retract.

Back in her room, she looks for paper and pen, but the Econo Lodge doesn't provide stationery. She tears a page from her court notebook, keeps the message short and cryptic, doesn't sign her name. If F-17 should overlook the note she is about to slip under his door, and Cornrows's boyfriend's sister should find it while she is cleaning tomorrow, the note will prove nothing.

Tonight was our last night, it reads.

The minute she slips the folded note under his door, she starts waiting for his response, even though the note was a statement, not a question.

She opens the thriller her husband recommended. Had she slipped that same note under her husband's door thirty years ago when they first started their affair, her husband would have taken it for what it was: an invitation.

She skips breakfast the next morning so that she isn't tempted to have a cigarette with F-17.

In the van ride over to the courthouse, she engages in a conversation with the schoolteacher, who Skyped last night with her dying uncle in his hospital room. It takes a force commensurate with pressing two opposing magnets together to keep her mind on the schoolteacher's sorrowful description of her ravaged uncle. F-17 sits on the schoolteacher's far side. C-2 doesn't understand why this quiet man with his bad skin and inability to decipher an invitation in a denial has taken up so much of her thoughts.

In the jury room, C-2 continues to avoid him, joining the church lady and the alternate on the sofa. She registers the church lady's chatter as distant birdcalls.

As she files into the courtroom two places behind F-17 and takes her seat, her stomach growls. She is annoyed with herself for not eating anything on the first morning of testimony. One more reason she made the right decision to end the affair.

Tim Rush, Stephana's boyfriend and the state's only eyewitness, takes the stand. He is short, sinewy, buzz-cut, and he clenches his jaw as if he were biting down on rawhide.

The prosecutor's opening questions are gentle.

Tim—Timmy to his friends—grew up with his single mother in Ocala, attended Forest High School. Tim calls the prosecutor "sir" and the judge "ma'am." He admits to a bumpy childhood and a stint in juvy. He credits his turnaround to Stephana, Jesus, and Mr. and Mrs. Butler. He met Stephana when Mr. Butler brought his Mercedes into the garage where Tim worked as a mechanic. He would define his relationship with Stephana as "real serious." He says he knows what the prosecutor means by "intimate," and the answer is yes.

C-2 opens her notebook and writes:

1st. Stephana 2nd. Jesus

She looks over at F-17's notebook. He has already filled his page.

The prosecutor asks Tim to tell the jury in his own words what happened on the afternoon of the fire.

"I punched out of work fifteen minutes early so Steph and me could make a movie. We were meeting up at her house first."

He has told this story so many times by now that his tone is rote and rapid.

C-2 writes:

delivery sounds closer to an auctioneer than to a hero

"I pulled into the Butlers' driveway around five. I was going to wait in the truck for Steph to get home from Popeyes when Anca comes screaming out of nowhere and starts banging on my window. 'Fire!' she yells. 'Where's Caleb?' I ask. She's all hysterical like. I see flames in the nursery window. I grab my fire extinguisher and try to save the baby. I had to kick down the nursery door. It was stuck or something."

The prosecutor interrupts Tim's affectless delivery. "What did you see when you entered the nursery, Tim?" he asks in a fatherly voice.

"The baby was on fire," Tim says. "I aimed the hose and sprayed him with that foamy stuff. I was scared that stuff might be poisonous, but what else could I do?"

"How long did you remain in the nursery after you realized that Caleb was dead?"

"Couple of seconds."

"Where was Anca?"

"Outside, waiting for me. I told her Caleb was dead. It was like she didn't hear me, so I said it again."

"How did Anca react to the news of her brother's death?"

"She ran off to see if her dogs were okay."

F-17 has flipped open his notebook to a previous page, the one with the large block letters: *SMOKE? BEFORE LUNCH.*

. . .

After Gladys takes the jurors' orders, F-17 asks C-2, "Cigarette?"

"I'm quitting," C-2 says.

"You should try the patch," Cornrows says, rolling up her sleeve to reveal a nicotine Band-Aid on her stringy bicep. "I'm quitting, too," she says.

Without taking his pleading eyes off C-2, F-17 sits back down again. "I guess I'm quitting as well," he says.

On the two-minute ride back to court, he sits beside her. Her need to talk to him presents itself as a ringing in her ears.

Once in the jury box, she opens her notebook and focuses on her pencil point, but she accidentally presses down too hard and snaps the lead.

The defense counsel's opening questions for Tim aren't nearly as gentle as the prosecutor's.

"Why do you keep a fire extinguisher in your truck, Mr. Rush?"

"I used to be a volunteer fireman," he says, but he sounds confused, as if he isn't sure if he should be proud of this past service, or if it will sink him. He looks beseechingly around as if for someone to guide him. Stephana? Jesus?

"When did you stop being a volunteer fireman?"

"Year ago."

"Why?"

"Steph wanted me to go to community college."

"You were acquainted with some of the volunteer firemen at the scene?"

"Yes."

"Would you characterize them as friends?"

"I knew them from around, but I wouldn't say friends."

"Around where?"

"Baseball," Tim says.

"Didn't you play in a league with some of these men?"

"Yes."

"When did you purchase the fire extinguisher?"

"I don't remember."

"Your credit card statement says you purchased it three weeks before the fire."

"I guess if that's what it says," Tim says.

"Four weeks before the fire, didn't you ask Mr. Butler for a loan to open your own garage and he turned you down?"

"Yes."

"Did Mr. Butler eventually set you up in business?"

"Yes."

"When was that, Mr. Rush?"

"Three months ago."

"After the fire?"

"Yes."

C-2 wishes she hadn't broken her pencil so she could write down what the defense counsel has left unsaid—that Tim started the fire with the intention of rescuing Caleb so that in gratitude Mr. Butler would reward him with a loan, or, better yet, his own garage.

The defense counsel uses up the rest of her time bulleting her argument—Tim knew where the accelerant was kept because he helped Mr. Butler paint the nursery; he smoked cigarettes and would have had matches. But her main point is made, and C-2 doesn't have a workable pencil to jot it down. Another validation of her decision to end the affair.

The prosecutor's rebuttal is simple. "Tim," he asks, "when you pulled into the driveway on the afternoon of the fire, did you see Anca running out of the burning house?"

"Yes," Tim says.

.   .   .

In the van, on the way back to the motel, the deputy announces that tonight's dinner is at Red Lobster. He asks for a show of hands for takeout.

C-2 waits to see what F-17 will do. Whatever he does, she will do the opposite.

He hesitantly raises his hand, while his eyes implore her to lift her hand too. When she doesn't, he continues to stare at her with questioning eyes.

At promptly 6:30, C-2 joins the other jurors for the interminable meal at Red Lobster.

.   .   .

Though it isn't yet nine o'clock, she has already entered the fugue state as the microcrystals of Ambien erase notions of time and space. She has no idea how long she's been asleep when she hears her door open and close. It is so dark with the blackout drapes shut, she can only locate him by the sound of his breath. Without the benefit of sight, his body language comes to her tactilely. She can sense his unabashed hurt and the small bravery it took to plead his case.

" 'Tonight was our last night'?" he says. "Did you mean what you wrote?"

Her husband would never have asked that tiresome question, for which there never is an answer.

He stands by the door waiting for her reply. "I don't know what this is, but I know we can't stop," he says.

She finds him and kisses him. With Cornrows in the adjacent room and the church lady below, they have silent sex, which turns out to be even sexier than noisy sex.

After he leaves, C-2 turns on the light. She needs to write a note to herself in case the Ambien prevents her from remembering what just happened.

The only paper she can find is her court notebook. She hesitates before desecrating court property with her dear-diary entry. She might as well crib a line from the new translation of Madame Bovary.

I have a lover!

A flat-screen monitor is positioned in front of the jury box. The prosecutor inserts a time-stamped DVD of Anca's confession, which he has been arguing to admit for the past hour. The date is two weeks after the fire.

C-2 rallies all her focus and humanity to listen and watch as if it were a matter of life or death, which it is.

Anca sits alone in an interrogation room. Her hair is black, her bangs at half-mast. If she is worried, her body language doesn't reflect it—no fidgeting, no twisting a hank of hair as she did during the prosecutor's opening statements. Her blinking, too, seems within the range of normal.

The interrogation room door opens and Anca's head revolves at the same incremental speed that C-2 witnessed before. An overweight detective with unusually long arms and a rolling gait comes into the small room. He plants his hands on the table across from Anca and leans over her.

"Anca," he says, "we know it was arson."

He then disappears from the frame and sits—or stands—behind the camera.

The choice of where to place a camera in an interrogation room may seem immaterial to the other jurors, but not to C-2.

Had the camera been behind Anca, had the screen been filled with the threatening body language of the detective, Anca's mumbled admissions might have look coerced.

C-2 starts to write *detective's POV* when she sees the words, written in her own hand though she has no memory of writing them: *I have a lover!*

By the time she recovers her concentration again, Anca has already confessed.

.   .   .

At Nic & Gladys, F-17 tells the deputy he's going outside for a smoke.

Cornrows opens her purse and offers him a nicotine patch.

"Thanks, but no thanks," he says. "I'll quit after the trial."

C-2 rises from her chair. "Me too," she says.

Cornrows makes her the same offer.

"You're a stronger woman than I," C-2 says.

Outside, he asks, "May I come back tonight?"

She wishes he wouldn't ask permission.

"I'm not paying attention in court," he confesses. "If I know I am going to see you later, I'll be able to listen. We both will."

The logical mind that had conjured up the syllogism during the *voir dire* is scrambling.

Inside the restaurant, Nic carries out the first servings. C-2 realizes that everyone has been watching them through the window. She grinds out her cigarette. Gladys arrives with a plate of peas, collards, and rice just as C-2 joins the others.

"How come you never eat the main course?" Cornrows asks.

"I'm a vegetarian," C-2 says.

"Does it help you lose weight?" asks the church lady.

"I don't know, I stopped eating meat when I was five," C-2 says.

"Your parents allowed that?" the church lady says.

"I *hated* vegetables as a kid," Cornrows says. "What did you eat?"

"French fries."

In the van, he sits behind her. She can practically feel his breath on her neck.

.   .   .

The flat-screen monitor is still facing the jury box when C-2 and the others file in.

A volunteer fireman takes the stand. He acknowledges that he filmed the footage the jury is about to see. He was making a training film when the alarm went out. He had no idea he was filming a crime scene.

The court's lights are dimmed to make allowance for the overexposed amateur footage.

Six firemen, shouldering axes, jog the perimeter of a large Spanish-style house, searching for the source of the smoke, which is thick. The camera pans, and C-2 spies an almond-shaped flame in a window. The nursery window? The camera turns around and films two men attaching a nozzle to a hydrant while a third man uncoils a length of hose from the truck. Why is the jury being shown this footage? Then C-2 understands. Tim is now in the picture—you might even say he is the star. He is the only man without a helmet and fire-retardant gear. Bareheaded, in his street clothes, he charges into the burning house first.

She glances over at F-17. In the darkened courtroom, the firelight is kind to his bad skin. His eyes look so intelligent and thoughtful as he studies the footage.

When the lights come back on, C-2 worries that one of the other jurors might have seen her staring at F-17, until she notices that everyone is staring at the church lady, whose head is lolling. She has dozed off.

An arson expert takes up the remainder of the afternoon, explaining the chemistry of combustion. C-2 pays strict attention, though the effort it takes is proportionate to running a race while balancing an egg on a spoon. She doesn't understand any more about what the expert is saying than she did when she took high school chemistry and had to repeat the course in summer school. The teacher finally gave her a pity C.

She writes:

pyrolysis of solids
exothermic reactions
gasification equation

By the time she finishes phonetically sounding out the words in her head in order to spell them, she has forgotten the definitions—just like in high school.

To pay attention to something you don't understand when there is such an alluring narrative waiting to take over your thoughts proves undoable. The only clear memory she has of last night is the silence of the sex. The arson expert refers to a back draft as a "vacuum of air," and the words "vacuum of air" become synonymous with the way she thinks about the implosion of her breath last night. The arson expert leads the jury back in time, room by burning room, to the origin of the fire, but C-2 keeps getting lost in the motel room. He came to her just before dawn. He must have been awake all night, planning his entrance. Or did he wake up and surprise himself, as he had her?

All she remembers after three hours of testimony is that there is no scientific test that will determine whether the arsonist used a disposable diaper or a pile of rubbish to start the fire.

I t's Friday night at TGI Fridays. Alcohol is allowed during dinner as long as the jurors pay for their own drinks. The mood is
celebratory. Tomorrow their families are visiting.

C-2 orders a martini. She misses her husband terribly, but she
doesn't miss helping him fill his pillbox every morning and then
crawling around the kitchen floor to find the pills he has dropped.
If she is honest with herself, she dreads his arrival.

After dinner, as they are smoking near the restaurant entrance
in sight of the deputy, F-17 says, "You never answered me. May I
come over tonight?"

"My husband will be here tomorrow," she says.

"I'll be gone by then."

She could say, *You knew I was married.* But she loves her husband
too much to conscript him into her mendacity.

"I'll come to you," she says.

To wait in her bed for her lover to arrive is one thing—more an
acceptance than an act. To sneak out past midnight, open his door,
and feel her way across the carpeting to his bed is quite another.

He is already erect.

Is this why she's here, to remember being desired that badly? To feel her sexual power again?

An erection in an octogenarian is less a manifestation of desire than a celebration of life and modern medicine.

After sex, she can sense his need to talk, the postcoital sharing that lovers do.

"Is this the first time you've slept with someone since you've been married?" he asks. His tone isn't flirtatious. He sincerely wants to know if he is her first affair. As she suspected from his lovemaking, he is developing a tenderness for her, and that isn't why she's here.

She strokes his face to put a salve on what she says next. "I don't want to talk about my marriage, and I don't want to know about your girlfriend."

"I don't have a girlfriend at the moment," he says, but his tone is light again.

He gets it. She thinks he gets it.

To change the subject, she asks, "What age were you when you decided to cut up bodies for a living?"

"I'm not a serial killer," he says, "I'm an anatomist."

"Did you own a Visible Man as a boy?"

"Visible to whom?"

"A see-through man with plastic organs?"

"I didn't want to be a doctor when I was a boy. I wanted to be a musician."

"What instrument?"

"My voice."

"Were you a choirboy?"

"My parents were both psychiatrists who believed that religion should be listed as a disorder in the *DSM*."

"Were you talented?"

"I thought so."

"What changed your mind?"

"Stage fright. My acne. The Talking Heads. I saw them in concert when I was fifteen."

C-2 saw them in concert when she was thirty. She is grateful that he chose a band she has heard of. Had he chosen a band that she didn't know, she would have been prepared to lie.

"About halfway through the concert," F-17 continues, "Byrne began slapping his head each time he sang the refrain, *same as it ever was.* The knock on his skull gave his voice vibrato. It sounded as if these were his last words. I knew that no matter how much I practiced, no matter how many hours I trained, I would never be that creative, that uninhibited."

He sings in a near whisper, *"Same as it ever was, same as it ever was,"* and on the third chorus he slaps his forehead.

She can't see him do it in the dark, but she can hear how the slap changes his voice, from clarity to stupefaction, crediting the refrain with an illusion of profundity.

"That was beautiful," she says.

"I can only perform like that because you can't see me."

She imagines him at fifteen, the aspiring singer in the throes of acne. A drooping lid is hardly the equivalent of erupting pustules, but she has an idea of what it cost him.

She touches his face again, reading the pitted skin like Braille. His lack of guile, and the leftover scars, and his precocious understanding of his own limitations cracks open her resolve to forbid herself feelings for him, a crack in the teacup that opens a lane to the land of the dead, according to Auden.

. . .

Saturday morning, the Prius pulls into the Econo Lodge parking lot. Her husband exits the car with a shopping bag.

He shields his eyes against the low sun to search the parking lot for her, where they had agreed to meet. C-2 remains behind the blackout drapes in her room, waiting for the elderly man with the flyaway white hair to transmogrify into her husband.

"Hey," she calls to him from the second-story walkway, but he doesn't appear to hear her over the interstate din. The open door of the Prius catches the sideways glare of the sun. He squints in every direction but hers until he finally spies her crossing the parking lot.

"I thought maybe I had the wrong motel," he says, hugging her.

She walks him to the office so that he can register with the deputy.

"I have to show ID to visit my wife?" he says, signing the form.

As they pass the ice machine, he says, "Could they have chosen a more dreary motel?"

Outside F-17's door, her husband says, "I missed you so much."

She opens her door without a key.

"We can't lock the door?" he says.

She starts to open the blackout drapes.

"Leave them closed," he says.

They sit on the twin beds facing each other. The reading lamp is on. She notices a large bruise on his elbow.

"Did you fall?"

He looks at the bruise in surprise. "I must have banged my elbow during the night. Does it feel hot to you?" he asks, offering her the bruise.

She gingerly touches it. "Does it hurt?"

"You know you're old when you look and feel like the morning after but there was no night before. I come bearing gifts," he says.

Using his sandaled foot, he slides the shopping bag closer and hands her the first surprise, a set of white, six-hundred-thread-count Egyptian cotton sheets. He fishes out a week's supply of chocolate, trail mix, and power bars, and her swimsuit, waterproof iPod and earbuds, and her AquaJogger.

Looking at her gifts, she fights the urge to confess. If she confessed, where would she position the camera? Behind her, so that only her husband's face is in the frame? Or behind him?

They strip the bed together, the one she sleeps on, not the one she uses as a table.

They undress and get under the new sheets, but they don't kiss. They talk. Conversation has always been their foreplay. She asks how his memoir is going.

"Remember the time in Bamiyan? You went off to photograph the cliffs where Taliban blew up the Buddhas."

"I went off to photograph the unemployed people who had been the Buddhas' caretakers."

"And I went to the prison made of mud. Anyway, I ditched the warden and got lost and stumbled across a cell with a tiny hole. I looked through it and saw a young girl, maybe thirteen years old, lying in a heap facing the door but with a totally blank stare and nothing else in the cell with her but a blanket and a cot. No sink, toilet, or anything to distract her. I freaked out and got my interpreter and the warden and asked what she was in jail for. He explained that her father had brought her there because she ran away with her boyfriend and their families caught them and then they ran away again. I asked why she had no water and why she was kept so isolated—wasn't that cruel? He said yes, he felt very bad for her, but there were no female prison guards, so they had to keep her isolated like this without much human contact until a female police officer came by twice a day. He wished they had a female prison guard to take care of her."

"Just write it exactly as you told me," C-2 says.

Only an hour remains of the visit. It is time to make love. The familiar domesticity takes over. Each gets up for a last urination.

They kiss and touch, but he doesn't get hard. "I feel like I'm on the clock," he says. "You know I want you," he says. "I can hear people talking outside. The bed is too narrow. These sheets are too slick. I think the words 'conjugal visit' did me in."

She waves goodbye to him from the second-story walkway. If she had her camera, what would she focus on? The splayed fingers flattened against the Prius's window in a parting gesture, or the pink updrafts and mile-high purple thunderheads rumbling over the Prius with a tiny starfish in the window?

.   .   .

C-2 has said many forgettable things about photography during the occasional lectures she gives at art schools and universities, but she will never regret saying this: Art is a conversation.

In her twenties, when she photographed rock stars and socialites for *Interview* magazine, she thought the conversation was supposed to be witty, and sexy, and hilarious, and beautiful, above all else, beautiful, the kind of beauty that inspires adoration.

When she met her husband and became a photojournalist, the conversation turned to ethics, and beauty was no longer supposed to inspire love: it was an agent for goodness.

When that conversation became only righteous noise, she started photographing animals, relishing caws, hoots, and bellowing. It took a few months, but she finally learned to distinguish what the bellowing meant. Animals have their own conversation.

Lately, she has been taking pictures without her camera. Blinking instead of clicking. Why does she need to provide proof of what she sees? Lately, she has begun to suspect that the conversation—the wit and the dogma—was all in her head, like a person who talks to God and to whom God talks back.

She leans against the railing. Far from city lights, the night sky is both beautiful and sublime. During her lectures, she explains the difference between the beautiful and the sublime this way: The stars are beautiful—diamonds, twinkles, something you can wish upon. The space in between the stars is the sublime—cold, black, and infinite, something that inspires awe and fear.

She envisions her elderly husband waving goodbye from the Prius this afternoon. Does that image inspire love, something she can wish upon—or awe and fear that the most difficult part of her life is just beginning?

At breakfast, a Sunday brunch catered by IHOP, the ex-military reads a message to the jury from the judge. The court is treating the ladies, and the gentlemen if they would care to join them, to a manicure and a pedicure this afternoon.

"They'll pay for a pedicure and not our drinks?" says the alternate, reaching for the maple syrup.

"Will they pay for a bikini wax?" asks Cornrows.

"Did you know you can get an STD from a bikini wax?" the church lady says.

"I don't think that's possible," F-17 says.

"It is if the waxer double dips," the church lady says.

"Show of hands for the pedicures," the ex-military says.

Everyone but F-17 and C-2 enthusiastically raise their hands.

"Have fun," C-2 says. "I think I'll take a swim instead."

She puts on her bathing suit, the black tank that her husband brought her yesterday, grabs the AquaJogger, but not the waterproof earbuds and swim-pod (she wants to hear F-17 coming, if he comes), and heads to the shaded pool. The sun will not reach it for another hour.

She is very aware that the bulky sky-blue flotation belt ages her.

At least the pool is in the shade. At least she isn't a middle-aged Florida matron in an AquaJogger wearing zinc block, sunglasses, and a sun hat.

C-2 normally enters a pool by the steps or the ladder, but today she plunges in—she needs the silence and compression of water, the few seconds where nothing above the surface matters. When she comes up for air, she clips on her flotation belt and begins running. Suspended in the deep end, she runs as fast as she can. The water resists her, defies her: the sensation is like trying to catch a train in a dream. If she were on dry land, she would be running a six-minute mile.

He arrives with his towel and goggles and beautiful feet.

"Do you have an injury?" he asks.

The question confuses her until she realizes that he thinks the exercise is therapeutic.

"I deep-water-run by choice," she says. "There is a great lesson in running as fast as you can and not getting anywhere."

The ex-military, who lost the rock-paper-scissors wager to his partner and had to stay behind to keep an eye on them, sits upright on a chaise lounge less than ten feet away.

"You should have brought your bathing suit," C-2 calls to their guard. "At least take off your shoes and put your feet in the water."

"I wish," the deputy says.

"Will my swimming laps disturb you?" F-17 asks her.

"When you are running nowhere, nobody gets in your way," she says.

As he passes her on his first lap, a leisurely warm-up crawl, his hand purposely brushes against her thigh on the downstroke. On his way back, hand and thigh meet up again. Back and forth, hand and thigh. She only slows her stride when his fingers reach her.

The sun has entered the deep end. Under the surface, the light creates spectral patterns of wavy luminescence. Above the water, the sun is brutish.

One of the pleasures of deep-water running is that she can close her eyes. Only with her eyes shut is C-2 released from the ceaseless dictate to find the right image. She can't locate him by his splashes alone, and the anticipation of his touch is what she runs toward.

When she finally opens her eyes again, the world incrementally develops before her, from overexposure to pastels to brassy color, like an old-fashioned Polaroid. She unclips the electric-blue belt, tosses it onto the deck, and swims to the shallow-end steps. She towels off, collects her belt, waves a general goodbye, and strolls up to her room, all the while trying to ascertain, without turning around, if F-17 will be following.

She peers out from behind her blackout drapes. F-17 is trapped in a conversation with the deputy, who has finally taken off his shoes and socks and is dipping his feet in the pool. Why oh why did she have to suggest that he soak his feet? Now he is going to sit there all day.

When she looks out the drapes again, less than five minutes later, F-17 has left the pool area, but the deputy has not. He sits soaking his feet with an unobstructed view of the second-story walkway connecting F-17's room to hers. She hears a door close, and a second later, a single rap on their shared wall.

She taps back.

Two sharp knocks respond.

It takes a few rounds, but she thinks she finally understands the pattern. Her room has the better view of the pool. One tap means *No, don't come over, the deputy is still watching.* Two taps mean *Yes, the deputy is gone.* A simple but adequate binary language.

An hour later, the deputy is still soaking his feet and their tapping has become babble.

The voices of the returning jury silence them. The next knock C-2 hears is on her door. Cornrows is rounding up an audience.

"Come check out our pedicures," she says, ushering F-17 and C-2 to the lobby. Beside the front desk, the other jurors are modeling their newly painted toenails for the ex-military who had to stay behind and the old Indian woman who appears to man the front desk ceaselessly.

The church lady's toenails are conventional red. The schoolteacher flashes a glint of gold. The chemical engineer's nails are clear lacquer, Cornrows's powder blue. The alternate hikes up his pants and waves his toes, his maroon nails pointing in every direction.

"We're all going to play Trivial Pursuit before dinner," Cornrows informs the new arrivals.

C-2 tries to bow out, but Cornrows pouts. "You never want to join in. Come on, it's more fun with more people."

At the long folding table off the lobby, the six of them divide into three teams—Cornrows and the church lady, the schoolteacher and the alternate, and F-17 and C-2. The chemical engineer has excused herself to take a nap.

The die lands on yellow, F-17 and C-2's team color.

The first question is read by the deputy: "Who painted the *Mona Lisa*? A. Van Gogh. B. Michelangelo. C. Da Vinci?"

Ostensibly to discuss their answer in private, the yellow team retreats to the farthest corner of the lobby.

Out of earshot, F-17 says, "I'll be there as soon as everyone goes to sleep."

"Yes," C-2 says, but she finds herself emphatically shaking her head no, as if to pantomime a heated argument about who painted the *Mona Lisa*.

The church lady theatrically coughs. The others are impatiently waiting for their answer.

"Time's up," the deputy calls to them. "Who painted the *Mona Lisa?*"

"Da Vinci," C-2 says.

Team blue is up next.

"How many colored balls are there in billiards?"

The alternate and the schoolteacher confer.

"Fifteen," the alternate says.

Next is green.

"What religion was Adolf Hitler?"

The church lady and Cornrows confer.

"Mormon?" guess the ladies.

"Catholic," the deputy corrects them.

The yellow team is up again. "Which nail grows fastest? A. Pinky. B. Middle. C. Thumb."

F-17 and C-2 retire to their corner.

"Why did you shake your head no? Should I come or not?" he asks.

Why must he ask?

"Time's up!"

"Middle finger!" F-17 yells across the room.

"I'll come to you," she whispers.

Her husband's sheets are still on her bed.

. . .

Just after midnight, she steps outside to see if the deputy is around, and if the other jurors have all retired. The lights are out in every other room. Shutting the door quietly behind her, she reaches for F-17's doorknob when she spies the alternate less than twenty feet away. He stands next to the ice machine, sucking on a cube, wearing only his boxer shorts, barefoot, his lacquered toenails ten tiny moons refracting the overhead spotlight. Moths swoop around him.

She jerks back her hand. He flashes her a licentious grin.

"I guess I have the wrong door," she says, idiotically.

Back in the room, her pulse is banging so loudly that she isn't sure whether or not she hears the single rap on the shared wall. She is too shaken to dare answer it.

Before breakfast the next morning, lighting her cigarette in the parking lot, he says, "I waited all night for you."

"We've been seen," she says. "Last night, outside your door."

"Who?"

"The creepy alternate."

Cornrows finds them in the parking lot.

"Can I bum a cigarette?" she asks.

The news trucks are back in force. A full-size charter bus from the Villages has replaced the minibus. The line of spectators waiting for a seat at the Anca Butler trial has doubled since last Friday.

"What's going on?" the church lady asks the deputy as the van descends into the parking garage.

"You know I can't answer that," he says.

"Maybe Anca's going to testify?" Cornrows speculates.

"Not unless she's going to testify against herself. The prosecution hasn't rested," the chemical engineer says. "Stephana must be next."

"The twin? How do you know?" the church lady asks.

"Why else the hoopla?"

Hanging back, F-17 catches C-2's sleeve as the jury crowds into the garage elevator. He says, "We'll take the next one."

As soon as the elevators doors kiss, he asks, "Do you think he's going to say anything? What did he see exactly?"

"My hand on your door."

On the ride up, the elevator stops on the first floor. A group of seniors bull in. From the furtive exchanges and smiles of recognition, C-2 realizes that the jurors in the Anca Butler trial have become minor celebrities, the talk of the Villages. She wouldn't be surprised if the old gentleman in the elastic-band jeans asked for her autograph.

In the jury room, she avoids F-17 lest they be overly conspicuous after the private elevator ride up. The alternate hasn't taken his eyes off her. She braves a moment alone with him.

"I guess you couldn't sleep either," she says, joining him on the sofa.

"It was a real hot night."

"Almost woke up Doc"—F-17's nickname among the jurors— "by mistake."

"Lucky I was there," he says, grinning as he had last night.

. . .

The chemical engineer was right. Stephana takes the stand. She hasn't been in court since the *voir dire*. Someone has instructed her to still her animated eyes and sweep up her blond hair, so that the jury has a full view of her exceptionally beautiful face. C-2 can't help but compare the sisters. Where Anca's cheeks are pudding, Stephana's are bone.

C-2 notes that the sisters haven't yet acknowledged each other. Stephana is too busy glancing around the gallery. Anca's stare is drilled to the floor.

"Did Anca tell you that she started the fire?" asks the prosecutor after Stephana is sworn in.

Stephana looks defiantly at her sister, demanding that Anca acknowledge her, but Anca refuses to raise her eyes. C-2 isn't sure how, but the sisters are communicating.

"Yes, she told me she started the fire."

"Did you put those words in Anca's mouth?"

"No."

"How long after the fire did Anca confess to you?"

"That night," Stephana says, explaining that the fire was out by the time she got home, that Tim was sitting on the curb, crying. "He told me Caleb was dead and that Anca had started the fire. Tim didn't know where she was," Stephana continues in response to the prosecutor's prompts, "but I knew she'd be with her dogs. She'd locked herself inside one of the kennels. She was threatening to kill all her dogs and then herself."

C-2's gaze ping-pongs between the pudding cheeks and the bones. Only when Stephana looks directly at the jury, full-face, to tell them that Anca wished Caleb had never been born, does C-2 understand why the twins look so different. Anca's nose is asymmetrical, Stephana's is perfect.

"What was Anca's demeanor when you found her in the kennel?"

"Anca doesn't have a demeanor."

"Did you ask her if she started the fire?"

"I didn't need to. She told me she started it but that Caleb wasn't supposed to die. She was supposed to rescue him."

"Why would she put her brother in danger only to rescue him?"

The defense objects, but Stephana is allowed to answer. "She'd done stuff like this before. She would make her dogs drink hydrogen peroxide so they'd vomit and then she'd nurse them back to health."

"Did she tell you why she made her dogs sick?"

"She said she did it so that Mom and Dad would think the therapy is working. What I mean by that," Stephana clarifies, "is that Anca's in treatment to learn how to empathize. Anca's on the spectrum."

"What spectrum is that?"

"The autism spectrum."

"Do you think Anca loved Caleb?"

"Objection," says the defense attorney, who has been writing notes on her yellow pad to Anca, who doesn't read them. Anca is sneaking another chocolate bar.

"Did you love Caleb?"

Stephana's symmetrical face erupts into wet chaos.

"Yes," she says.

C-2 looks over at Anca, who has finally raised her eyes and acknowledged that her twin is on the stand. The leaden eyes in the blank oval are the diametric opposite of Stephana's *Sturm und Drang.*

C-2 writes:

identical or fraternal?

.   .   .

"Identical," Cornrows says, lighting her after-lunch cigarette with F-17's last match.

"They don't look all that alike," C-2 says, lighting her cigarette with Cornrows's burning tip. "Stephana's nose is sharper."

"Environment factors in," F-17 says, using C-2's cigarette to start his. "Even in utero, one twin takes up more space. If soft tissue, like nose cartilage, is pressed against the uterine wall, the shape can be influenced."

"Anca's right-handed and Stephana's a lefty," Cornrows says.

"How do you know?" C-2 asks, unable to conceal her surprise at Cornrows's astuteness. C-2 is a northeastern snob, despite having grown up around Vegas, in a fourplex, aluminum foil taped over the windows to keep cool. Her mother had risen from even poorer prospects, a trailer, and had stunned the family when she rose to become a blackjack dealer. Cornrows reminds C-2 of her mother, that same mix of chattiness and wile.

"Anca twists her hair with her right hand and Stephana twirls hers with her left hand," Cornrows replies.

"They're mirror-image twins," F-17 says. "They come from a single egg, but the egg doesn't split in two right away. The two fetuses develop reverse asymmetric features—right- and left-handed, birth-marks on opposite sides, or hair whorls that swirl in opposite directions."

"Does that mean one twin is good and the other is evil?" Corn-rows asks.

. . .

"Let's talk about that night," the prosecutor says as soon as Stephana settles back into the witness chair after lunch. "You said you came home from your afterschool job at six. You work at Popeyes. What is your job at Popeyes? Do you manage only the drive-thru window? Do you normally work till six? Where was Tim at that time? I'm going to show you a diagram of your house. Could you point out where Tim was? Could you point out where the firemen were?"

It is like listening to a crazy relation tell you everything, I mean everything, about their day. "I took the bus home. It stops on 441. Tim and I were going to see a movie. In Ocala. I think it was *Horrible Bosses*. I don't remember who picked the film. I think it started at 6:40, but Tim likes to watch the previews."

The glut of facts has caused C-2 and the other jurors to grow sleepy after the heavy lunch, all except the alternate. He is scribbling away. From C-2's vantage point one chair above him, three chairs to his left, she can almost see his notebook. As if to relieve a crimp in her neck, C-2 stretches and steals a peek at his open page. It is black with doodles of naked women. But not helter-skelter breasts and buttocks. He has begun with a tiny naked woman dead center, then drawn an outline around her, and another around that, and another and another, a woman inside a woman inside a woman, like an X-ray of Russian dolls.

Is his whole notebook filled with naked women, or did he only start doodling them after he caught her trying to sneak into F-17's room?

.   .   .

After seven hours of Stephana's testimony, and with another mati-
nee performance tomorrow, the jury unanimously votes to return
to the motel and order takeout. The seven of them have run out of
small talk and can no longer abide one another's company without
alcohol.

In the motel lobby, as the jury recites their menu orders to the ex-
military, a complicated roundtable of indecisions and specificity—
raw not grilled, no ice, extra Thousand Island—C-2 and F-17 slip
away, racing through the parking lot.

They kiss behind the dumpster, then light up cigarettes, like teen-
agers, but Cornrows finds them.

"I didn't mean to freak you out," she says at their startled reactions.

What did she see?

Does she know?

Did the alternate tell her?

Will she tell the church lady?

Will the church lady tell the deputy?

Will the deputy tell the judge?

Will C-2 tell her husband?

Cornrows sticks out a beggar's hand.

"I promise to buy my own pack tomorrow," she says.

As C-2 sits in her room that evening, picking at the microwave-
soggy vegetarian fajitas, she doesn't practice eating alone. She is dining with F-17, separated only by a quarter inch of gypsum board.

S how me how you dissect a body," she says.

"So that's your secret fetish," he says.

C-2 is supine. She reaches for his hand in the dark and uses it to draw a Y-shaped line from under each breast up to the sternum and then the throat. "Is this how you begin?"

"That's if you're performing an autopsy, searching for a cause of death. A dissection isn't only about how someone died, it's about how someone lived. The bodies arrive in two shrouds, one for the body, the other for the head."

He covers her with the sheet.

"The medical students have never seen a dead body before. We ask them to remove only the body shroud. A couple of students always break down."

He slides the sheet off her.

"We ask them to roll the body prone."

He rolls her over.

"We start with the back, the most impersonal part of the body, to help the students adjust. We make a series of cuts, divide the back into four equal sheets of skin."

He draws, very lightly, a line from the base of her skull to her buttocks, another from scapula to wing. He draws a third and fourth along the lateral edges of her body from under her armpits to her hips.

"We lift off the skin."

"Is there blood?"

"No blood. They've been embalmed, a light embalm, just a little formaldehyde. Next we move to the upper arm and shoulder."

He rolls her supine again, and lifts her arm, folding it gently behind her head.

"The armpit is ticklish because it's one of the most sensitive places on the body. All the sensations in our fingertips must pass through it on their way to the brain."

He draws a line along the path of those sensations.

"Next we examine the hand."

He lifts hers and traces its bone structure.

"My students get very emotional when they first examine the hand. A hand, in its own way, is as personal as a face. Some of the hands are still wearing nail polish. It's the first time my students truly realize it is a human being."

He puts down her hand.

"It's time to open you up," he says.

"Do you crack the chest?"

"No, we saw the bones laterally, remove the sternum with ribs in one unit."

"What do you see first?"

"The lungs."

"Not the heart?"

"The heart is buried in the mediastinum, enclosed in a sac of fluid to keep it safe while it pumps. The heart is only attached to the sac's posterior wall by veins and aortas. They anchor the heart to the body while allowing it a lot of flexibility to move around, like a dog on a leash. Otherwise, it might wander off."

After he finishes with her heart, he wants to have sex again. She knows he can't accept that there is no future for them beyond this room. At fifty-two, she has a different kind of sexual power than she had at twenty-four. She doesn't like this new kind of power one bit, but she also can't get enough of it.

The court registrar reminds Stephana that she is still under oath. It is the defense attorney's turn this morning.

"Yesterday, you told the prosecutor that you and Anca kept a journal together," the defense counsel says, holding up an old-fashioned leather-bound diary marked with a blue sticker.

C-2 has no memory of Stephana testifying that she and Anca kept a journal. She was too preoccupied watching naked women proliferate in the alternate's notebook.

"Did you each write your own entries?"

"No," Stephana says. "I wrote my own, and Anca dictated hers to me."

"So the journal contains only your handwriting. Could you read us the underlined entry dated three days prior to the fire?" She hands Stephana the journal, open to a marked page.

"I will light a match," Stephana reads, *"and walk back the way I came, touching it against the wet places. At first the flames will be pale and eager, then they will become yellow with bits of red. I will let the flames grow tall, even to the nursery window, so that the danger will be at its highest before I rush in to save Caleb."*

"Is that your handwriting?"

"Yes, but I only wrote down what Anca told me to."

"Are you familiar with a short story called 'The Heroine' by Patricia Highsmith?"

The prosecutor objects. The attorneys squabble. A sidebar is called.

"Didn't you write an essay about 'The Heroine' for your AP English class?" the defense counsel continues after the judge gives the okay.

"Yes."

"Would you read us the underlined passage from 'The Heroine'?" The defense counsel hands Stephana a Xerox of the story.

"*'Then she lit a match,'*" Stephana reads, "*'and walked back the way she had come, touching it against the wet places. . . . At first the flames were pale and eager, then they became yellow with bits of red. . . . She would let the flames grow tall, even to the nursery window, before she rushed in, so that the danger would be at its highest.'*"

"Anca's not in your AP class, is she? Anca doesn't take AP classes, does she? Isn't Anca in a special program for students with learning disabilities? You're asking us to believe that she memorized a paragraph from a story you wrote a paper on and then dictated it to you? Could you tell us what the story is about?"

Another objection, row, sidebar.

The judge recesses court so that she can retreat to her chambers to read the story. Fifteen minutes later, she's back, a coffee stain on the Xerox printout. She rules that the jury will not get to hear the plot, but they will get to hear the three paragraphs preceding the cribbed diary entry.

"*'If only there were a flood . . . ,'*" the court register reads in an affectless voice. "*'She imagined the water coming higher and higher around the house, until it almost rushed into the nursery. She would rescue the children and swim with them to safety.*

"*'Or if there were an earthquake . . . She would rush in among fall-*

ing walls and pull the children out. Perhaps she would go back for some small thing—one of Nicky's toys—and be killed! Then the Christiansens would know how much she loved them.

" 'Or if there were a fire . . . Fires were common things. There might be a terrible fire just from the gasoline that was in the garage . . .

" 'She poured some gasoline on a corner of the house, rolled the tank further, and poured some more. She went on like this until she reached the far corner. Then she lit a match and walked back the way she had come, touching it against the wet places . . .

" 'At first the flames were pale and eager, then they became yellow with bits of red. Lucille began to relax. She would let the flames grow tall, even to the nursery window, before she rushed in, so that the danger would be at its highest.' "

. . .

"Was Lucille autistic?" asks Cornrows, during lunch.

"Who's Lucille?" asks the church lady.

"The heroine of the short story," says the chemical engineer.

"Aren't heroines always supposed to be good?" asks Cornrows.

"That's the irony of the title," says the chemical engineer.

"Are you talking about the daughter?" asks the church lady.

"Lucille wasn't their daughter," Cornrows says. "She called them 'the Christiansens.' "

"You're not allowed to discuss the trial," warns the deputy.

"We're discussing a piece of fiction," says F-17.

"What I'd like to know is why we aren't allowed to hear the story for ourselves," says the schoolteacher.

"I don't get it either, why does the judge keep us in the dark?" asks the church lady. "Aren't we supposed to find the truth?"

"I warned you," says the deputy.

"We're not discussing the case, we're discussing why Justice wears a blindfold," says F-17.

"We're only allowed to hear evidence that can be proved," the schoolteacher tells the church lady.

"How do you *prove* the plot of a story?" asks Cornrows.

"What the fuck are we discussing here?" asks the alternate.

"You don't have to be so crude," says the schoolteacher.

"You don't have to be such a cocktease," says the alternate.

"I want him removed from our table. I won't sit with him," the schoolteacher tells the deputy.

"Watch yourself," the deputy warns the alternate.

"Fuck yourself," says the alternate.

"The judge is going to hold you in contempt if you don't shut your pie hole," says the deputy.

"I'm already in jail, what the fuck worse can happen?"

"Can we please eat in peace," says the church lady.

"I'm not sitting with him," the schoolteacher reiterates to the deputy.

"Me neither," says Cornrows.

"Nic," the deputy calls to the older West Indian man at the fryer. "Could you set up another table and chair?"

"You putting me in the corner?" says the alternate.

"I want to return to the courthouse," says the church lady, rising.

"Me, too," says Cornrows.

"Go ahead and wait in the van," says the alternate. "I haven't finished eating."

"Nic," the deputy says, "bag up all the leftovers, they can finish eating in the jury room."

"Mind if we go outside for a cigarette?" F-17 asks, rising from his chair along with C-2.

"Not today," the deputy says.

Back in the jury room, no one finishes their lunch except the alternate. The schoolteacher sits by herself on the sofa, in tears. C-2 walks over. Despite the saucy outfits, the schoolteacher is a sweet, modest young woman. She must have gotten her courtroom dress code from TV, where female attorneys always show cleavage.

"When is this going to be over?" the schoolteacher asks C-2.

"As soon as the prosecutor rests, we'll be at the halfway point," C-2 says.

"We're not even halfway?"

C-2 can only think of platitudes. She tests one. "Is it really so bad?"

"Maybe not for you. You seem to be having a good time."

C-2 is struck mute.

The schoolteacher knows.

Who else knows?

As the jurors file into the courtroom to take their seats, C-2 assesses each one. The church lady suppresses a yawn. The chemical engineer slips off her flats and slides them neatly under her chair with her bare feet. Cornrows turns around to shoot the alternate a contemptuous glare. The alternate glares back, then shifts his eyes to C-2 and winks.

They all know.

. . .

"Tim painted the nursery, so I guess he knew where my dad kept the turpentine," Stephana answers a question that C-2, still shaken by the wink, didn't catch.

"How long was Tim a volunteer fireman?"

"Three years."

"He must know an awful lot about fires."

"I don't hear a question," objects the prosecutor.

"Did you purchase a bottle of hydrogen peroxide a week before the dogs got sick?" asks the defense counsel.

"I don't remember."

"Let me show you the receipt."

Stephana studies the receipt sealed inside an evidence bag.

"If I bought it, it was for Anca. She always kept a bottle in the kennel's first-aid kit. Last summer, her dachshund ate a sago nut and died."

For the first time since the trial started, Anca reacts to what is being said. At the mention of her dachshund, she covers her face.

C-2 writes:

Anca is capable of love

That evening, when they meet outside the restrooms at Olive Garden, C-2 tells F-17, "They all know."

"You're sure?"

"Yes."

"Did someone say something?"

"He winked at me in court. They know."

In the pool after dinner, she tells him about her exchange with the schoolteacher. The mosquitoes have chased the ex-military back into the lobby. "I said, 'It's not so bad,' and she said, 'Not for you. You seem to be having a good time.'"

"That little shit told her," he says, dogpaddling beside her.

"He told everyone," she says, remembering the alternate's wink.

"All he saw was you reaching for the wrong door."

"By the time he's done embellishing, he'll have seen me giving you a blowjob by the ice machine."

They reach the deep-end wall and turn around. His face is lit from below by the pool lamp. In this watery, playful light, his skin looks unblemished. He is handsomer with smooth skin, but not as sexy.

"Do you think someone will tell the judge?" she asks.

"Tell her what? That the alternate, who draws dirty pictures all day, claims he saw you going into my room? I'm more worried someone will gossip with the deputy and he'll make it his job to watch us more closely."

"Can we be thrown off the jury?" she asks.

"We didn't take an oath of celibacy."

"Still," she says, "this judge said she threw someone off a jury for just looking up a word. Do you remember the word?"

" 'Prudent.' "

They reach the shallow-end steps and turn around, only to see the deputy standing by the deep end, swatting at his ear.

"Time to call it a night," he tells them. "You're not getting bitten up?" he asks.

"Mosquitoes don't like chlorine," F-17 says.

As they towel off, she whispers, "Is it true mosquitoes don't like chlorine?"

"I made it up. I'm being eaten alive," he says.

"Don't come tonight," she whispers, as they mount the stairs up to their rooms. "It's too risky."

Around two a.m., after they make love in his bed, she says, "One of them is going to tell the judge for the same reason children always tattle to the teacher. For attention and a gold star."

"We can't be the first sequestered jurors to have a love affair," he says.

His choice of the words "love affair" startles her. She would characterize what they are having as a fling. Or would she?

She says, "At the very least, the judge will order us to stop."

"Am I going to see you after the trial is over?" he asks.

"After the trial is over, C-2 won't exist," she says.

Stephana has prepared herself for her cross-examination this morning by wearing no makeup except a dusting of pancake over a smear of antiperspirant, a trick C-2 learned during her portraiture days. The antiperspirant discourages the brow from sweating, and the pancake blots up any overflow.

C-2 wonders if the "natural" look was the prosecutor's idea or that of Stephana's mother, who has been sitting in the courtroom every day in a fresh coat of makeup. Her skin is so pallid around the edges of her sun-beige foundation, and her eyes are so dry and dead beneath her blue-shadowed lids, the makeup looks applied by an undertaker. She slips a chocolate bar to Anca before the gavel is hammered. C-2 plans to spend a portion of the cross-examination studying Mrs. Butler to see which of her daughters she believes.

The flat-screen monitor is wheeled back into the courtroom. The defense counsel has her own movie to share. As the lights dim, she explains to the jury that the video they are about to watch was shot on Stephana's iPhone six days after the fire.

In jeans and boots, Tim combs through the charred rubble of the Butler home. Only the screened-in pool and the free-standing three-car garage are intact.

Stephana's voice is the soundtrack. "You're standing where his office was."

Tim looks around, lifts the remains of a chair.

"You see Dad's safe?"

"No, but I found this," says Tim, holding up something large and black and egg-shaped.

"It's your dad's smoker," Tim says.

"Maybe we should make BBQ tonight," Stephana says.

Tim laughs, but Stephana's laughter is closer to the microphone and drowns him out.

The courtroom lights come back on. Mrs. Butler's face has paled to such a colorless pallor that her sun-beige foundation now looks like mud.

"Did you shoot this video?" the defense counsel asks Stephana.

"Yes."

"On your iPhone?"

"Yes."

"Is that your voice?"

"Yes."

"Why was Tim looking for your father's safe?"

"Because Dad asked him to. The safe was fireproof."

"What was in the safe?"

"Dad's important papers."

"Anything else."

"Mom's jewelry."

"Was the safe ever recovered?"

"Yes."

"Was your mother's jewelry inside?"

"No."

Mrs. Butler's dead eyes fill with water. The inflamed red rims can't hold back the overflow. It rains down her cheeks, forming creeks in the mud.

She doesn't know which of her daughters to believe any more than C-2 does.

.   .   .

"Can't we have lunch someplace other than Nic and Gladys?" asks Cornrows as the van pulls out of the underground parking lot. "It's always so fattening."

"You don't need to lose weight," says the church lady.

"I like their fried chicken," says the alternate.

"Nic's got a contract with the court," the deputy explains, pulling up to Nic & Gladys.

While the jury finishes their lunch of fried tilapia with rice and canned corn, C-2 and F-17 step outside for a smoke.

"Should we keep meeting like this? In front of everyone?" she asks.

"If we stop now, they'll know that we know they know," he says.

She knows she shouldn't ask the next question. It's one thing to have sex with another juror, another to discuss impressions of a witness, but she is so curious to have his take on what she just heard she can't resist. She asks, "Didn't Stephana's laughter sound demonic to you?"

"Her laughter sounded like a release to me," he says. "I hear that kind of dark humor all the time with my students."

"That wasn't dark humor," she says. "That was morbid."

"Laughter is a defense mechanism. It helps us cope with the idea of our own mortality."

"I don't think Stephana believes she's mortal," she says.

Cornrows pushes open the restaurant door, an unlit cigarette between her lips. She opens a fresh book of matches, strikes, and exhales into the sun. "Thank you guys for refusing to finish your lunches," she says. "Maybe Nic will take the hint and stop with the prison food."

Does she know? C-2 wonders.

Late that afternoon, the prosecution rests his case, surprising everyone. His last witness, a pontificating police officer who wasn't even at the crime scene, is only there to refute the defense's innuendo that Stephana stole her mother's jewelry. There were two other burglaries in the neighborhood around the time of the fire.

C-2 was expecting the prosecution to close with a motive. Some explanation, no matter how preposterous or simple-minded, as to why the affectless teenager who loved her dachshund set her eighteen-month-old brother on fire. C-2 is always skeptical about the role of causality in human impulses, the way Hollywood reduces a serial killer's motives to a flashback of a psychotic mother putting out her cigarette on the serial killer's eight-year-old palm. But to offer no theory? No dénouement?

To the midway point," toasts the schoolteacher, holding up a glass of chardonnay. The jury is celebrating at Applebee's. It's Friday night. The trial is half over. Tomorrow their loved ones are visiting again.

"Isn't it also called the point of no return?" asks the church lady, ordering a hamburger that the menu promises is *"slammed with flavor."*

"I thought the point of no return meant it was too late to pull out," says the alternate, ordering the twelve-ounce sirloin with peppercorn sauce.

"I warned you about being vulgar in front of the ladies," says the ex-military, ordering the fiesta lime chicken.

"The point of no return is the moment when continuing a journey becomes less dangerous than turning back," says F-17.

· · ·

That night, on the spare bed in her room, he asks her to describe one of her photographs for him.

He wants to talk now before sex. That is her husband's and her exclusive foreplay. But he is insistent.

She chooses a picture from her portraiture days. A reclusive actress had agreed to be photographed for *Interview* magazine after fifty years of avoiding the camera. She was eighty-seven. C-2 had expected to find Gloria Swanson from *Sunset Boulevard,* but what she found instead was an unkempt old woman who had forgotten how much she hated the camera. She had also forgotten to comb the hair on the back of her head before she sprayed it in place. It flared out.

"'Could you make me look beautiful?' she asked me," C-2 tells him. "Did you make her look beautiful?"

"I photographed her in profile, by a window, silhouetted against the sunlight, so that her features are more suggested than present. Let people remember how beautiful she was. In the photograph, her white hair flies backward, as if she is traveling at great speed."

She realizes that they are crossing the point of no return, though not in the way he defined it earlier, as the moment when continuing a journey is safer than going back, but in the way the alternate defined it, as unstoppable.

After he leaves, she strips the spare bed, puts the sheets outside the door, then pulls them back inside lest the alternate make another trip to the ice machine.

She takes a shower and lies down. Her husband will be here in less than six hours.

. . .

The Prius pulls into the parking lot. The door swings open and her husband exits the car without a gift bag this time. C-2 remains in her room, concealed behind the drapes, watching. A strong wind is blowing and a dust devil chases him across the parking lot. He walks as quickly as he can. Something about him in motion, with his cane, seems cantilevered. Wrists, elbows, shoulders, knees, all snap to as if operated mechanically, with great economy. He has objectives. He heads to the office to sign himself in, climbs the stairs, passes the ice machine and F-17's door.

Last night, F-17 told her he preferred to be alone today.

Her husband has only two speeds—full throttle and low gear. At parties or out to dinner with friends, people only see him in full throttle and marvel at his energy. But she knows his low gear, after all that exertion has drained the battery. He sleeps during the drive home. He can barely undress himself before bed.

The plan this morning, which they discussed on one of their twice-weekly Skype sessions, is that she will wait for him in bed, naked.

Touch me, remind me who I am, wrote Stanley Kunitz, in her husband's favorite poem, not just because of the language, but because Kunitz wrote it at ninety.

Her husband slips into her room. He doesn't speak, as they had agreed. She pretends to be asleep, as they had agreed. He undresses, slides under the new sheets he brought last week, holds her tightly, spoon-fashion. He kisses and fondles her, but he doesn't get hard.

He sits up, baffled as to why an eighty-six-year-old man doesn't get an erection at the snap of his fingers. That intrepid bafflement, the lunacy and the hope of it, is the essence of who he is. He says, "I don't understand. I took a pill. I think it's because we can't lock the door. Anyone could just walk in. This room gives me the creeps."

He props himself up on an elbow. She rolls onto her back.

"How much longer will you have to be here?" he says.

"The prosecution rested yesterday," she tells him. "Maybe another ten days?"

"You made CNN, Nancy Grace."

"I wish you wouldn't watch news about the trial."

"Why?"

"Because you have information the jury isn't supposed to hear."

"So? I won't tell you."

"But it drives me crazy that you won't tell me. *Is* there something the jury should know?"

"I won't tell you."

"Then why bring it up?"

He tries to touch her, but she jerks back.

"Watching news about the trial makes me feel close to you," he says.

"Nancy Grace inspires closeness?"

"It's so dark in here with the blackout drapes shut," he says. "I can't see you."

"You want me to open them?"

"No."

The conjugal part of the visit is ruined. They might as well nap together. As she nestles against him, and feels her husband's lap against her buttocks, his chest against her back, all the bones and bumps couple together in practiced, comforting compression, like an old mattress whose imprint you naturally fill.

"Are you lonely?" she says in her full voice. He won't be able to hear her if she whispers.

"Of course I'm lonely."

"Any more dizzy spells?"

"I don't want you to worry."

"Are you wearing the Lifeline?"

She can feel by his deadened weight against her back that he has fallen asleep. She closes her eyes. The nap is more intimate than sex.

She waves goodbye to him, the tiny starfish in the window of the Prius under the enormous sky. Only today, there are no thunderheads. The sky is sunny and blue and ridiculously hopeful.

S unday brunch at Cracker Barrel. The weekend deputy, the state-fair beauty queen, reads a text from the judge offering the jury two possible diversions for the afternoon: a field trip to the Ripley's Believe It or Not! museum or bowling.

"My vote is for bowling," says the church lady, sprinkling Tabasco on her grits.

"My kids will get such a kick out of me going to the oddatorium!" says Cornrows, poking her hash browns with her fork to see if they are crisp like she ordered.

The beauty queen confers with the ex-military, and they agree to split up the jury, but only if everyone participates in one activity or the other.

"Must we?" asks the chemical engineer.

"You can't be alone at the motel," says the beauty queen, "and there are only two of us."

"Please," the schoolteacher pleads with the chemical engineer, "I can't stand another second in that motel room without a TV!"

In the end, the chemical engineer agrees to join the bowling crowd. Cornrows will accompany F-17 and C-2 to the museum.

Since there are only three of them, the deputy takes her squad car. F-17 rides shotgun, C-2 and Cornrows sit in the back, behind the wire mesh protecting officers from the perps. At every stoplight, Cornrows waves to people in the adjacent cars.

At the museum, the beauty queen leaves them on their own so she can talk on her cell with her mother—she has told the three of them she is getting married next week.

At the front counter, thronged with tourists, C-2 and F-17 try to ditch Cornrows while she collects brochures to give her kids. The museum is packed. Bumper-to-bumper strollers. Families are being funneled through a twisting maze of poorly lit exhibits—shrunken heads, the iron lady, a two-headed-calf skull, a wax figure of a giant-ess shrouded in dust. Someone has stuck a piece of chewed gum on her elbow.

In the crush, he pulls her to him, places his hand around her rib cage just below her breasts. He starts to guide her into an unlit nook for a kiss.

"I found you," says Cornrows, coming up behind them.

She accompanies them past a backlit X-ray, a human skull tipped backward with a beam of white light piercing it. It takes a moment before C-2 realizes she is looking at a radiogram of someone swallowing a sword.

"Is it real, Doc?" asks Cornrows.

"Appears so," says F-17. "Swallowing a sword isn't all that hard. The trick is to linearize the oral cavity as much as possible by leaning the head way back, and then pushing the base of the tongue forward. That's probably the trickiest part. All of this causes the oral cavity to become a relatively straight shot down to the base of the skull. The other trick is to use a very dull sword."

Must he give such a thorough explanation and waste so much time?

While Cornrows peers through a microscope to read the Lord's Prayer on a grain of rice, they finally lose her again and find themselves in an empty theater playing a documentary about Robert Ripley's life. The officious narrator's voice, combined with the barrage of freakish life, and his hand on her thigh, and the starfish in the Prius window, and the crib on fire have all melded together in this dark theater.

"I'm falling in love with you," he says.

Cornrows makes her way to their row of seats. She whispers to C-2 and F-17, even though the three of them are the only ones in the theater, "He was once voted the most popular man in America."

"Who?" asks C-2.

"Ripley," says Cornrows.

The film ends, only to begin again. The three of them exit together, pass the frozen-shadows exhibit.

"Let's take a picture," says Cornrows.

"Of what?" asks C-2.

"Our shadows," says Cornrows, pressing a pulsing red button.

C-2 is momentarily blinded by a flash. On the wall behind are three frozen shadows that they can step away from without disturbing. Cornrows's shadow is waving. F-17's shadow is turned toward C-2, his hand extended. C-2 is in profile. Silhouetted, she doesn't look all that different from her portrait of the old actress.

What is she doing?

. . .

He wants to talk about their future. He didn't tell her what he told her this afternoon without expecting a response.

"I wish we could smoke in this room" is her response.

"I meant what I said," he says. "I'm in love with you."

They have not yet had sex. He is lying on top of the covers, fully dressed. Blind in the darkness, she reaches over and strokes his face.

"You know, you always touch my face before giving me bad news."

"Do I? It's my only way of seeing you in the dark."

He sits up. The twin mattress sighs as he rises. "I wanted to live in the dark as a teenager until I realized that ugliness already makes you invisible," he says.

"What does that mean?"

"You touch my face *not* to see me."

He gets up to leave.

"Please don't go," she tells him.

"Do you have any feelings for me?" he asks.

"My mother told me that I should never sleep with a man I didn't love but that I could be in love with someone for a night."

"It's been thirteen nights," he says, but he returns to bed so as not to waste the fourteenth.

C-2 thinks, The point of no return is long past. The point of no return is now a vanishing point on the far horizon, the point that is supposed to put the picture into perspective. All lines lead away from it.

But where do the lines lead after they exit the frame?

C-2 settles into her chair in the jury box on Monday morning, and glances at the gallery to see which members of the Butler family have come to support Anca on the opening day of her defense. Mrs. Butler is there, as she is every day. Beside her sits Mr. Butler, a concave soul who looks pithed of spirit. This is his first day in court since the *voir dire*. He sits directly behind Anca, but avoids looking at the back of his daughter's pageboy by staring at the acoustic-board ceiling, his wife's profile, the flag. Next to him sits the grandmother, a blonde in her mid-eighties. C-2 recognizes her. She has been in court before, but C-2 had assumed she was a member of the "watchers"—the jury's nickname for the seniors from the Villages.

The defense counsel calls her first witness, a forensic psychiatrist with a front-loaded Ivy League CV and a new haircut, who specializes in the psychology of false confessions.

"What else but guilt," asks the defense counsel, "would cause an innocent person to confess?"

The psychiatrist starts with statistics. Out of two hundred persons on death row whose convictions were overturned by DNA evidence, one-quarter had falsely confessed. He cites another study, Bedau and

Radelet, which identified three hundred and fifty wrongful convictions for capital cases, forty-nine of them caused by false confessions. He offers more fractions: two-thirds of innocent confessors are mentally ill; one-third have IQs lower than seventy; two-thirds think if they confess they can go home.

To C-2's right, the church lady releases a disconcertingly loud snore, then snaps back to alertness.

"False confessions are categorized into three types: voluntary, coerced-compliant, and coerced-internalized," continues the psychiatrist. He defines each term in laborious, jargon-clotted verbiage.

The church lady's head nods forward. C-2 waits a moment to see if she will wake on her own, then reaches over and stirs her shoulder.

"Why did you interrupt me?" the church lady says. "I'm not asleep, but it doesn't mean I'm awake."

Halfway through the psychiatrist's list of reasons why an innocent person might confess—delusion, a morbid desire to attract attention, a passionate impulse to unburden the conscience—the church lady falls asleep again.

This time C-2 decides not to surreptitiously wake her. Instead she raises her hand to attract the attention of the bailiff. He walks the length of the jury rail so that C-2 can whisper her request to him without disrupting the proceedings.

"May we take a short coffee break?" asks C-2, nodding in the direction of the church lady, who is fighting to stay awake and not sure of what is going on.

The bailiff approaches the judge. She covers her microphone and he covers his mouth, as if a great secret were about to be told. The judge glances at her watch.

"Let's take an early lunch," she says, then turns to the church lady. "Eat lightly."

During lunch, the church lady self-consciously picks at her

food—fried pork chops with macaroni and peas. Cornrows, C-2, and F-17 watch her through the window during their smoke break.

"She'd been sleeping all morning. I didn't know what else to do," C-2 says.

"You did the right thing," F-17 says.

"She told me she didn't sleep all last night because of the pain," Cornrows says. "She hurt her back bowling."

After lunch, the church lady returns to the courthouse with a lidded cup of coffee. The bailiff allows her to bring it with her to the jury box, but she doesn't know where to put it.

"I wish we had cup holders," she says to no one in particular.

The forensic psychiatrist returns to the witness chair, and the judge reminds him that he is still under oath. The prosecutor begins his redirect. Despite the prosecutor's heft, he is springy and combative in his polished shoes.

"Let's look at your statistics again," he says to the psychiatrist. "How many false confessions are preceded by sleep deprivation? What is the percentage?"

"About 75 percent."

"How long was Anca's interrogation?"

"I would need to see the police report."

"Less than an hour?"

"Yes."

The church lady's head falls forward yet again. It bobs and sways in C-2's peripheral vision. The judge notices as well, stops the proceedings, and asks the bailiff to please wake up juror number four. As he approaches the sleeping woman, his footfalls are the only sound in the court. He clears his throat loudly, then calls, "Juror number four."

When the church lady regains consciousness, every eye in the courtroom is on her.

Without singling her out, the judge addresses the jury. She

reminds them that they took an oath to try this case according to the evidence, and that means they must remain alert in order to properly follow the evidence. She explains that she has some concerns that not everyone has been able to follow the evidence. She asks if any of them has had such a difficulty. When no one raises their hand, she addresses the church lady.

"Do you believe that you followed all the evidence?"

"Yes," says the church lady.

"You weren't asleep during any of the testimony?"

"My eyes were closed, but I was listening," says the church lady. "I listen to books on tape with my eyes closed."

Both lawyers call for a sidebar. The lawyers talk at once, but it is only posturing. C-2 can sense that the brouhaha is only for the jury, that the judge and attorneys are all in agreement.

"Juror number four is dismissed," the judge says.

Stunned, the church lady is led away by the bailiff.

The alternate moves to the seat beside C-2. He winks at her. He is now the sixth member of the jury.

. . .

Two more witnesses take the stand that afternoon—another psychiatrist who specializes in autism and an arson expert who refutes everything the prosecutor's arson expert said. At this rate, the defense will soon rest its case. Who else can they call? Character witnesses? Anca's mother? She was Caleb's mother, too. Then the trial will end and C-2 will never see F-17 again. A dull panic thumps over the monotonous voice of the arson expert as he explains his very different conclusion about the fire's origin. In his opinion, the fire started in Stephana's room. The paint thinner splashed throughout the house was a diversion. Paint thinner was not the active accelerant.

"What do the burned eyelashes prove?" asks the defense counsel.

"The eyelashes prove that Anca didn't start the fire. They were singed by heat, not flames. Had she been at the origin of the flame, with all the accelerant the state claims she used, her eyebrows and bangs would have been affected too."

C-2 looks over at Anca. Her eyelashes are blond, nearly invisible.

When it is the prosecutor's turn, he whittles his cross down to one question.

"How long after the fire were the forensics done on Anca's eyelashes?"

"Two weeks."

The defense rebuts, "What is the growth cycle for an eyelash?"

"Between four to eight weeks, then there is the resting phase, which lasts about a hundred days. To put it another way, if an eyelash fell out it would take at least four weeks to grow back."

"So doing forensics on an eyelash two weeks after the fire would not change the results?"

"Not in my opinion."

"The defense rests."

. . .

She hears a loud clang, like metal striking metal. The ice machine lid? Thunder? An accident on the interstate? Then silence. Then another strident stroke. She locates the sound. It is coming from inside his wristwatch, which is ticking next to her ear.

They have just finished having sex.

This is their last night. Tomorrow closing remarks will be heard. They both agree that it would be unethical to sleep together during deliberations.

"Promise me you'll see me again when this is over," he says.

"I can't promise that."

"You can't or you won't?"

He pulls out and silently dresses. He should have grabbed her and kissed her. Her husband would have.

C-2 doesn't entirely believe the prosecutor as he recounts the events leading up to the fire during his summation. Is he too solicitous? Is there a note of self-righteousness in his tone? Is it what he dwells on, and what he leaves out? Is it his vanity, his polished shoes? And then she realizes why she doesn't believe him: he is telling his account in the present tense. Anca *soaks* the diapers in paint thinner. Anca *lights* the match. He leaves out all cause and effect. He offers no reflection. He never uses *because*. His presentation is staccato, a punch list of Anca's actions that night and beyond, which he reads off a pad. Anca *hides* in the kennel. Anca *confesses* in under an hour after being taken into custody. He finally reaches the end of his account, but it is so unsatisfying without a motive. C-2 prefers Patricia Highsmith's ending, where the murderess did it because she wanted to be loved.

The defense counsel speaks extemporaneously, never referring to her notes as the prosecutor had. "Dr. Gold testified that it is common for one twin to be dominant and the other submissive. In a healthy twin relationship, one twin dominates physically, in sports, say, the other mentally, in academics or people skills. But in an unhealthy relationship, one twin dominates both physically and mentally. When that happens in boys, the dominating behavior is almost always physical. But in girls, the dominating twin controls the submissive twin psychically, and often becomes the spokesperson for the twinship.

"We know little of Anca and Stephana's first four years. We have no medical records from that time, except the birth records. Anca's birth weight was 2.6 pounds, considerably lower than Stephana's 5.6. A low birth weight predicts submissiveness. Dr. Gold explained to you that even in utero, one twin initiates the majority of coinciding fetal movements.

"Anca's confession was coerced, not by the police, but by Anca's own sister, her identical twin, Stephana."

C-2 has been watching Stephana all morning. She is back beside her mother, who looks hopeful for the first time since the trial began, yet C-2 can see how shamed Mrs. Butler is by her hope. Stephana holds her hand. Stephana is taking the defense counsel's beating without a flinch.

Anca reaches for her third chocolate bar that afternoon.

Stephana sighs dramatically, and then points out to her mother that Anca is sneaking another chocolate bar. Whatever hope Mrs. Butler felt vanishes, and Stephana's face brightens.

C-2 is sure: Stephana may not have started the fire, but she is guilty.

. . .

"You can find the defendant guilty of first-degree murder, or second-degree murder, or, failing that, of a lesser charge, manslaughter," the judge instructs the jury. It is late Friday afternoon. "The primary distinction between these is intent. The law is designed to treat killing someone intentionally as more blameworthy than doing so without intent or by reckless indifference. Depraved indifference to human life is different from reckless indifference. If the jury finds

Anca guilty of depraved indifference, then you may disregard intent and find her guilty of second-degree murder."

With no more than this cursory explanation of the charges, other than a laminated handout listing them, and no direction by the judge on how the jury should comport itself during deliberations, the jurors retire to the jury room. It is two in the afternoon.

F-17 is the first to speak. He reveals that he has been on a jury before. C-2 is taken aback that he has never mentioned it. He tells the others that the first thing they did on his former jury was elect a foreperson.

"I nominate Doc," Cornrows volunteers.

"I second," the schoolteacher says. "Hands?"

C-2 hesitates. He has been avoiding her, or, when they must interact, behaving with aching formality ever since he wordlessly left her bed the other night after she wouldn't promise to see him again. She isn't sure she would like the new alteration of power if he became foreman.

Everyone waits for her decision.

She finally raises her hand along with the others, and he moves to the head of the table. The gesture seems oddly ceremonial, or maybe he just wants to get away from her—they had been sitting opposite each other.

He proposes that as the first order of business they review the charges so that everyone understands them.

"We don't need to study, Doc, we have a cheat sheet," says the alternate, holding up the laminated sheet.

First-degree murder (willful and premeditated)
Second-degree murder (intent)
Second-degree murder (depraved indifference)
Manslaughter (reckless indifference)

"Let's take a straw poll," suggests the schoolteacher.

"Yeah, maybe we can go home tonight," says the alternate.

"We are not rushing to judgment so that you can go home," F-17 admonishes him. "Which of the charges are we voting on?"

"We can decide what she's guilty of later," says the alternate.

"How many others want to take a straw poll?" F-17 asks.

Though C-2 agrees with F-17 that they should thrash out the charges first, she casts her vote with the others.

He neatly tears six pages out of the special pad provided by the court and passes them around. He empties a glass bowl filled with Hershey's Kisses, and everyone drops their folded page inside. He stirs the sheets around, lest anyone be able to tell whose vote belongs to whom.

He reads the votes silently to himself. The act of keeping everyone in unnecessary suspense annoys her until she sees his apprehension.

"Four guilty, two not guilty," he says.

She tries to catch his attention, so that they can exchange a shared look. Despite their own personal travails, they will have to work together to convince the others of a not-guilty verdict, or, if they fail at that, a hung jury. But F-17, in his new authority, has other duties.

He asks if everyone would be willing to reveal their vote.

Cornrows abstains, even after F-17 explains that they will know her vote by process of elimination.

"I just don't want to say it first," she says.

"Fine, I'll go first. Guilty," the chemical engineer begins.

"Guilty," says the alternate.

"Guilty," says the schoolteacher.

"Not guilty," C-2 says.

"Guilty," says F-17.

His disclosure is so astounding and disquieting to C-2 that the other jurors momentarily become frozen shadows, and she and he are alone at the table, under the bright squares of fluorescent light checkerboarding the acoustic-board ceiling.

His eyes are filled with hurt, yet the pupils are already hardening into recalcitrance.

"Who would like to explain the reasoning behind their vote?" he asks the others, but he looks only at her.

"Why don't you begin," she says.

"Fine," he says. "She confessed."

"I didn't believe the confession," she says.

"Why not?" he asks.

"The camera's placement was from the vantage point of the detective. The focus was entirely on Anca's face."

"She was the one confessing."

"That kind of close-up without context is manipulative. The detective could have been pointing a gun at her, for all we know."

"Are you implying that the detective was pointing a gun at her?"

"Of course not. It's only an example of how untruthful a picture can be. We are only allowed to see what the cameraperson wants us to see, and in this case, the cameraperson was also the interrogator."

"No one laid a hand on her. She was in there less than an hour. She wasn't deprived of anything. There was an open can of Coke on the table," he says. "Or do you think the police are doing product placement?"

"Look, I make my living standing behind cameras. A lot happens *behind* the camera."

"Supposition isn't the same as facts," he says, turning to the schoolteacher.

"I voted guilty because of the story by Patricia Highsmith," the schoolteacher says. "Anca used it like a manual on how to burn down a house."

"The prosecution never proved that Anca had ever read the story," C-2 says.

"It isn't your turn to speak," F-17 says.

The chemical engineer is next.

"My vote is for second-degree murder. The choice of accelerant and the fact that it was splashed around the house indiscriminately demonstrates both desperation and a low IQ. I haven't yet decided whether or not it was depraved indifference or intent."

"Guilty," the alternate says. "I think Tim and Stephana seem like good kids. I didn't like the way the defense attorney kept harping on the eyelashes. I burn trash all the time, and my eyelashes seem fine to me."

"Not guilty," Cornrows says. "But only because I didn't want to vote guilty on the first ballot. I have reasonable doubt about her being not guilty."

"Reasonable doubt means not guilty," C-2 says.

"Reasonable doubt is a state of mind," F-17 says.

"It is the standard of proof for convicting someone," C-2 says.

"We haven't yet finished discussing the evidence, and you want us to debate legal terms?" he says.

"You're the one who didn't want to rush to judgment," she says.

. . .

No one wants to go out for dinner. Pizzas will be delivered to their motel rooms.

When the Domino's guy knocks on C-2's door, she is taking a bath.

"Just leave it outside," she shouts from the tub.

When she finally retrieves the box and opens the lid, she finds the pie polka-dotted with pepperoni. She is about to run outside in her robe to catch the Domino's guy and tell him she got the wrong order when she hears the alternate complain that he didn't get any pepperoni.

Tomorrow morning she is going to wink at him, and he'll never know why.

She lets her pie grow cold. She has no appetite anyway. All she can think is, *He voted guilty?* How did she get him so wrong? Are people that unknowable? Who did she believe those beautiful feet belonged to? She accepts her responsibility. She ended the affair. Is his petulance a form of anger or anguish? Are they distinguishable? Why does she have to practically restrain herself from going to him now? How is he so confident about his verdict? *I can't stop thinking about you,* he had said, *I should be thinking about the trial.* She certainly isn't certain of her verdict. Maybe he is right? Maybe reasonable doubt is a state of mind, the only state of mind.

Before throwing the pie away, she picks off the pepperoni to feed to the feral cats. On her way to the pool, where a tabby and a tuxedo have taken up residency on the chaises, F-17 finds her.

"I'm sorry I acted like such a prick today," he says. "You're entitled to your opinion."

He offers her a cigarette. It is hard to read his expression in the restless underwater light from the pool. Lit from below, everyone looks haunted. When he lights her cigarette, his fingers hold the burning match a dangerously long time, and she has to blow it out for him. She isn't positive, but she is fairly certain that he is on the brink of tears. No one appears to be around. She reaches for his face, but he jerks away.

"I think we should tamp down the hyperbole," he says.

"What are you talking about?"

"Suggesting that the detective questioning Anca might have had a gun," he says.

"It was an example of what might not be in the picture, not an implication."

"That nuance might be lost on some of the jurors," he says, and leaves her to smoke her cigarette alone.

.   .   .

Back in the jury room, where coffee and bagels have been provided for breakfast, C-2 asks to see the video of the confession again.

The judge sends back a note, which F-17 reads aloud. "In order for you to view the video, the court will have to summons both attorneys and other pertinent court personnel. That could take some time, given that this is the weekend. Could the jury rely on their collective memories of the taped confession instead? Are they sure they need to see the video?"

"I don't need to see it," says the chemical engineer. "My vote is based on science. The origin of the fire has to be the nursery. She was the only one home."

"You said so yourself," the schoolteacher addresses C-2. "We'll never know what's behind the camera."

"How many want to see the confession again?" asks F-17.

Only C-2 raises her hand.

F-17 looks exasperated as he pens a note back to the judge. Whatever the note says, it takes up half a page.

The judge answers promptly: The jury must cease deliberations until after the viewing.

The schoolteacher walks over and sits disturbingly close to C-2, who is now alone on the sofa, shunned by the others. The schoolteacher says loudly enough for the others to hear, "I know why you are doing this."

"I'm doing this because I want to be sure before I send a teenager to prison."

"You're doing this because you had a fight with your boyfriend."

· · ·

It is after two when the jurors are finally marched back into court to watch the confession again. The flat-screen monitor awaits them.

Before the judge calls court in session, she waits for the defense counsel to give instructions to a man, presumably the defense counsel's husband, who is holding a screaming toddler. The prosecutor, texting under his desk, wears shorts with black dress socks and tennis shoes.

The video begins: Anca alone in the interrogation room; her head revolving in slow motion as the burly detective enters; his disappearance from the frame; Anca mumbling yes to his accusations. Finally, Anca's first full sentence.

"I did it."

"You did what?" asks the detective.

"I killed him."

C-2 doesn't remember hearing those exact words before. She remembers hearing "Yes" after the detective accuses Anca of killing her brother, but she doesn't remember Anca taking ownership of the act: *I killed him.* How had she missed that? She knows. The previous time she had seen the confession had been the morning after F-17 slipped into her shower and they had had sex for the first time.

"May we see it again?" C-2 asks the judge.

"Is that what all of you want?" the judge asks the jury.

F-17, as foreman, answers for the others, "No, we don't need to see the confession again."

Back in the jury room, F-17 asks if revisiting the confession changed any minds.

Cornrows raises her hand. "I voted not guilty, but I'm changing my vote to guilty."

"What made you change your mind?" F-17 asks.

"It was the Coke can. I didn't notice it the first time. I don't know why. I drink Coke. Anca didn't seem as scared to me this time. I mean, if a detective was waving a gun at you, would you take a drink of Coke?"

"Can we take another vote?" asks the alternate.

"I think we should discuss the evidence against Stephana and Tim first," C-2 says.

The schoolteacher loses it. "What evidence?"

"The fact that no one tested Tim's clothes for accelerant? The fact that it was Stephana's handwriting in the diary entry that mapped out the crime?"

"She was only copying a story," Cornrows says.

"Do you still not believe the confession?" the chemical engineer asks C-2.

"Let's tell the judge we got a hung jury," says the alternate.

"It's too early to call a hung jury," F-17 says.

. . .

That night, C-2 reads over the notes that she took during the trial. Page one, *somebody loves her.* Why had she written this? From what hidden need within herself did that sentence burble up? *Defendant blinks 68xs a minute.* Could Anca's rapid blinking have been a symptom of daydreaming, as F-17 suggested? Had Anca been daydreaming while the picture of the melted crib was passed from juror to juror? *The prosecutor has no idea why she did it.* Must there be a reason? C-2 has never before subscribed to the premise that human impulses have reasons. Why now? Because she is confused and has lost herself? Because she needs reasons? Because she needs to be compassionate to assuage her guilt over cheating on her husband? Because she had to have one last dalliance before she got too old? Because she had a fight with her boyfriend? Why did she imagine that expressionless murderess was capable of love?

She turns the page and sees why.

I have a lover!

Part Two

S o, what was the verdict?" her husband asks.

He has been waiting an hour for her, idling the car in the weed-rampant parking lot of an abandoned shopping center, a ghost mall, thirty miles south of the courthouse. After the verdict was read and Anca, expressing nothing but nothing, was frog-marched away between two female deputies, the jury was hustled out of the courtroom, into the unmarked van, told only that they would be driven to an undisclosed location where a designated family member or friend would be waiting.

"Guilty," Hannah says.

Two cars over, next to a small sinkhole and a sign that reads "Oy's Market," the other jurors exchange phone numbers, promising to stay in touch. No one has asked for Hannah's number. She has been shunned since deliberations. She looks to see who is meeting F-17, but his ride hasn't yet arrived.

When she doesn't elaborate on her one-word answer, her husband asks, "Of what?"

"Second-degree murder."

"Intent or depraved indifference?"

"Depraved indifference," she says. "The defendant wasn't mentally capable of intent, let alone premeditation."

She asks to drive, pretends she has missed driving these past two and a half weeks, but they both know it is because she can't suffer him behind the wheel with his narrowing vision and his not knowing where his feet are. She pulls into a convenience store nestled between the interstate and the on-ramp. When she comes out with a pack of Parliaments, he says, "You took up smoking?"

In the chain supermarket, selecting her dinner from the shameless displays of paradisiacal abundance—she hasn't seen fresh fruits and vegetables in seventeen days—what she really craves is a cigarette.

"Do we need eggs?" her husband asks, even though he has been home alone for seventeen days.

In the checkout line, as their choices wobble down the conveyor belt, she glances at the rack of tabloids. A photograph of Stephana, hooded in a hoodie, stares back from the upper right-hand cover of *OK!* magazine. "CAUGHT IN A LIE," the caption reads.

"How much coverage did the trial get?" she asks her husband.

"It's Florida," he says.

She opens the magazine to read the full story. Turns out, Stephana had tried to pawn a broach of her mother's last March, before the fire. Why wasn't the jury told? She flips back to the cover. The issue she is reading came out after deliberations had begun. A statement from the Butler family says the broach in question was given to Stephana by her grandmother. But a source close to the family told *OK!* that Mrs. Butler would do anything to keep her other daughter out of jail. The reporter's conclusion: The wrong twin is on trial.

"Was this the consensus?" she asks her husband.

"It sells papers," her husband says.

After they unload the groceries and stock the refrigerator shelves with enough food for a week, he says, "Let's go out to dinner."

On the way out of the house, she notices a ball of sheets on the sofa.

"Did someone stay over?"

"Jimmy. I didn't want to worry you, but my leg went to sleep and I couldn't wake it up. Jimmy drove me to the ER. The doctor said it was a TIA, a ministroke, nothing to worry about, but he also said we should test me if I start to feel dizzy or my speech starts slurring."

He smiles at her. The smile is false and rigid, closer to rigor mortis than joy. "Are both sides of my lips curled evenly? That's the test."

Now, when he wakes up confused and dizzy in the middle of the night, in addition to her running for a baby aspirin and water, she will have to remember to ask him to smile.

The elderly man who can't possibly be her husband turns off the living room lights.

At the Indian restaurant—she hasn't tasted spice in seventeen days—he asks, "Why do you think she did it?"

"It's not like reading a novel," she tells him, "where the characters have motives. That's why they call it fiction. Because in real life people do inexplicable things to each other."

"They lie and cheat," her husband says, "but they don't immolate an infant. What did the prosecutor offer as a motive?"

"Can we talk about something else?" she says.

She sees the hurt on his face. This is about as interesting as life gets when you sit alone in the woods all day writing your memoir, and she won't share.

"He didn't offer a motive," she says.

"That was risky."

"It's difficult to assign motive to the insane."

"Why didn't the defense plead insanity?" he asks.

"She wasn't *that* insane. Please, Hy, I can't bear to talk about the trial, it's all I've thought about for three weeks."

Despite her edict that they not discuss the case, she and her husband watch the eleven o'clock local news—the verdict is the lead story. Heavily powdered to combat the heat, a recent university alum who is working her way up from weather to crime tries to talk over the hoopla outside the courthouse earlier in the afternoon. In the background, a crowd of two dozen hold up handwritten signs that read "Somewhere a Village Is Missing 6 Idiots," "Jury Guilty of Stupidity."

"Who are these people?" her husband asks.

Hannah thinks that she recognizes a few faces from the courtroom gallery, among them the old guy in stretch-waist jeans who followed her into the staff elevator and practically asked for her autograph. His sign reads "Arrest the Jury." Why such belligerence now? Next to him, a young woman—his granddaughter?—has duct-taped her mouth shut, cut a heart-shape opening to breathe through, and lettered with a marker across her forehead "Silence for Caleb." But something else unnerves Hannah more than the vitriol. All the signs are the same size of white illustration board, and all the lettering is the same color, a muddy red-black.

"Look, someone came prepared with blank signs and poster paint," she says. "The protest wasn't spontaneous. Someone organized it."

"Please tell me the judge promised not to release your names," her husband says.

"Is she allowed to do that?"

"Yes."

. . .

Despite an Ambien, her own bed and pillow, the familiar weight of her husband beside her, she can't sleep.

What else wasn't the jury told?

She wakes up her tablet to find out.

According to the barrage of articles, the defense counsel had complained daily about the lack of time to go over evidence it claimed the prosecution had withheld. The judge ruled against the defense's attempt to admit, as evidence, a motion-capture animation of what the defense claimed had happened the night Caleb died. It was built of footage from security cameras in the adjacent neighbors' houses. The prosecutor called the footage speculative and irrelevant, an animated cartoon. After that hearing, the defense moved to have deleted texts from Stephana to her friends admitted. The expert who extracted the texts had read a few in court—among them, Stephana telling a friend that she was going to smother Caleb if he didn't shut up. The prosecution alleged that the texts were a distraction, and the judge agreed. The jury never got to hear Stephana's next text to Tim: *i gave c one of gran's codeens. come over.*

The prosecution read Tim's response, *LOL,* and claimed the text was a joke, a distasteful but harmless joke.

The prosecution also asked the judge to consider whether or not the defense violated witness sequestration rules after it was revealed that Stephana had been present in the courtroom during the *voir dire.*

Tim had an impressive criminal record—grand theft auto, battery—that was never revealed in open court. What had F-17 said about Justice's blindfold? Something about the lack of light awakening other senses. Had she known that Tim had a rap sheet, would she have changed her mind, again, and gone back to her original *not*-guilty vote, caused a mistrial, made Mrs. Butler grieve through another trial? She hardly remembers Tim's testimony—only that he clenched his molars and ranked Stephana over Jesus. Would she have remembered more of what Tim had said if she hadn't been distracted by the notes her lover had written to her in his jury notebook and then angled the page so she could read the words from one row back, two chairs over? F-17 was rigidly certain of himself during deliberations. When he read the observations he had written during the trial to establish a point, Hannah was astonished by the precision and specifics of his note taking. She also observed that he'd ripped out his notes to her before reading his meticulous annotations aloud.

. . .

Next morning, reading the local paper, her husband discovers that the *Orlando Sentinel* has petitioned the court to release the jurors' names.

Furious, he calls their lawyer and his closest friend, Lenny. The two men met almost fifty years ago, when Hannah had just turned three. Her husband was covering the Chicago 8 trial, and Lenny was Abbie Hoffman's lawyer. A perennial bachelor, Lenny disapproved of Hannah when her husband first introduced them. He had pegged her as one of those beautiful young women who use old men's vanity to catapult themselves up the ascent, nearer to the volcanic heat of power and the swag of renown. Only later, when Hannah's left eyelid sank to half-mast again, and her burnish dulled into adequate, was Lenny able to accept her.

"Lenny says the petition is most likely perfunctory," her husband tells her after he gets off the phone. "He reminded me that even the *Times* petitioned the court for the jurors' names in the Central Park jogger case, but they never released them. I'm writing a letter to the *Sentinel,* in any case."

Hannah can tell that her husband thinks his name still glitters with fairy dust, that the editor who wasn't yet born when he won his Pulitzer will recognize his byline.

He composes the letter all afternoon, reads her the final draft aloud. He cites the Casey Anthony trial after the judge released the jurors' names. One woman reportedly quit her job and fled the state because of death threats. Others were scared to leave their homes.

He doubles down with the Zimmerman jury, noting that even after a six-month community cooling-off period, the release of the names ruined lives. He closes with the rash of memoirs written by the O. J. Simpson jurors, accounts of stress and collapse.

.   .   .

After dinner, when she goes out for a pack of cigarettes, she offers to mail the letter. On the way home, she finds herself driving past F-17's house. It is eight o'clock, nearly dark, but she doesn't need to slow down to read the poorly lit addresses on the mailboxes. She already knows what his house looks like—modest, manicured. She looked it up on Google Street View earlier in the day.

The lights are on.

She parks across the street, under sword-shaped leaves. She believes that if she can just observe him, even from a parked car a hundred yards away, she will begin to understand why it is impossible for her to let go of this person with the bad skin and the beautiful feet.

Framed by a window, he is standing under a kitchen fluorescent facing the street. She can only see him from the chest up. Whatever his hands are occupied with below the sill doesn't appear to interest him.

She would swear he is staring at her if she weren't positive that the kitchen fluorescent has turned his window into an opaque mirror.

She takes out her cell. She has his number from the time she asked for it, less than a month ago, so that she might photograph a dissection during his Gross Anatomy class. She looks down at her screen, at his name, Graham Oliver, and his phone number tempting her to press the icon of an old-fashioned receiver and hear his voice. Would she hang up after that? He would know it was her. She yearns for a time, not too long ago, when you could hang up on your ex-lover anonymously.

When she looks up again, Graham is holding a cat. He never mentioned that he had a cat. Who took care of the cat while he was sequestered? She knows nothing about him. She puts her phone down, but she doesn't drive away. She smokes a cigarette and watches him stroke his cat, from one hundred yards away.

H er husband is at his desk when the doorbell rings Friday morning. Hannah is still at the kitchen table, her coffee getting cold while she wonders again, *Who took care of his cat?*

"Are you going to get it?" her husband shouts from his study, where he plays Solitaire for the first hour of his working day to calm his nerves and muster the stamina to shoulder his memoir another half page forward.

"Could you?" she calls back.

"I'm working," he shouts, though they both know he is reshuffling the deck.

"All right," she says, but by the time she enters the foyer her husband has opened the door.

A sheriff's deputy asks for her by name, Hannah Pilar, hands her a manila envelope, and abruptly leaves before she has a chance to ask what this is about.

The document inside is a "notice to appear" on Monday before the judge in the Anca Butler case.

"You know what this is about?" her husband asks.

"I assume it has something to do with the release of our names."

"Is everyone on the jury being summoned?"

"I would guess."

"It makes no sense. Why call the jury into court to release your names?"

"Maybe she's giving us a heads-up so we can flee the state."

. . .

Graham is seated in the front row of the gallery when Hannah enters the courtroom Monday morning. He doesn't turn around. He must know it's her, because the rest of the jurors are already seated, spaced apart on the gallery pews, as if they are about to take a written exam and the judge doesn't want anyone cheating. No one speaks. The bailiff points Hannah to the back row.

One by one, not necessarily corresponding to their juror numbers, they are summoned to the judge's chambers—the schoolteacher first, then Cornrows, next the chemical engineer, and the alternate, who grins at Hannah when he sees her. The chamber must have a secret back door, Hannah assumes, because no one ever comes out again.

Graham and she are the only ones left. He occupies the farthest seat. He must have been the first juror to arrive. Did he come early in the hope of having a moment alone with her, or was he upholding his status as jury foreman by arriving early? He has cut his hair: the Platonic ringlets have been shorn, the back of his neck is freshly shaved. His ordinariness astonishes her. Only after his number is called and he is almost at the judge's door does he allow himself a glance back at her. What does that look hold? Want? Hurt? Confirmation? Of what? Or maybe he is as astonished, as she had been, by the other's ordinariness.

He is in there a long time, longer than the others. He must have prepared a lengthy statement filled with syllogisms arguing the logic of keeping the jurors' names secret.

When it's finally her turn, the bailiff closes the chamber door behind her.

The judge's office isn't paneled with mahogany, as Hannah had imagined. The decor is therapist, MSW not MD—neutral blond couch, blond desk, a soothing abstract painting, and no hierarchy of chairs.

Both attorneys are present, but not the defendant. The blousy court reporter loads another roll of paper into her stenograph machine before reminding Hannah that she is still under oath.

The judge begins, "One week ago, I received this letter, which I've shared with both attorneys."

The letter is open on the judge's desk. It is handwritten. Hannah can't make out the signature, though she tries.

The judge reads, "I feel it is my duty as a juror and a citizen to report that two of my fellow jurors had sexual contact on more than seven occasions during our nights at the motel. I was very upset by how lightly these two jurors took their responsibility in such a serious case. I am willing to testify that I heard sexual noises coming from one or the other's motel room on six occasions."

Hannah can see that the letter is longer, by at least ten lines, but the judge stops reading.

"Did you have sexual relations with another juror?" the judge asks.

"Yes," Hannah says.

"Did the two of you ever discuss the case while you were alone?"

"No."

The defense counsel interrupts: "You never offered an opinion on how the trial was going during your pillow talk?"

"I'm asking the questions," admonishes the judge. She turns back to Hannah. "Did your relationship in any way determine or influence how you reached your verdict?"

The longer Hannah hesitates before answering, the more her answer will sound untruthful.

"I don't know," Hannah says.

"'I don't know' means 'yes' in this case," says the judge. "Let me put this another way. Did the juror with whom you were having a sexual relationship in any manner coerce your verdict?"

"No," Hannah says.

"I won't ask you anything specifically discussed during deliberations, so let me ask this generally: Did your sexual relationship impede or influence any of the other jurors?"

"You'll have to ask them," Hannah says.

"I have," the judge says.

. . .

Graham flashes his headlights, once, as she walks past his car in the underground garage. Her phone rings as soon as she shuts her car door.

"Follow me," he tells her.

She follows his car to a truck stop ten exits south on the interstate, parks between his sedan and a semi with a flat tire and a garland of retread around the axle. Graham opens her passenger door, sits beside her.

"You okay?" he asks.

The concern in his voice almost makes her unable to answer.

When she does speak again, she can already hear the girlish rise in her throat—as if in married life, her natural voice is contralto, but with him, her voice ascends to mezzo-soprano.

"You?" she asks.

"I never saw it coming."

"What did you say when she asked?"

"I said it was no one's business. Did you admit to the affair?"

"We were under oath."

"Who wrote the letter?"

"The schoolteacher," she guesses.

"The church lady," he says.

"But she was thrown off the jury."

"Exactly."

"Do you think the judge will declare a mistrial?"

"We both swore under oath that the affair didn't influence our verdict."

"I told the judge that I didn't know if the affair influenced my verdict."

"Is that what you believe?"

"How could it not be true?"

"We never spoke about the trial."

"We didn't have to."

"I miss you," he says.

"I drove by your house," she says.

"I knew you were close by."

The motel next to the truck stop doesn't provide blackout drapes as the Econo Lodge had, only gauzy curtains covering a view of a propane tank. The sun is low. They undress for the first time in daylight. He is flaccid. She stands more like a soldier than a seductress. She has never seen him naked, or he her.

They allow themselves a moment to stare unabashedly and without judgment. It no longer matters what each thinks of the other's nakedness—the pitted back, the flattening buttocks. It no longer matters if they disappoint or excite. This is the end of the affair.

Their sex is slow, methodical, comfortable, the closest they have ever come to matrimonial sex. Familiarity is always said to be the blanket that suffocates passion. But familiarity can also be passion's accelerant.

They lie side by side without touching. A thrumming fills the space. It must have been there all along, though Hannah is only now aware of it. The noise is coming from the woods, insects rubbing one body part against another. The indifferent ceaseless rubbing speaks of life eternal, the insects that will be there long after she and Graham have gone their separate ways, after the motel has gone bankrupt, and the woods have taken over, after her husband has died, and her own vision has narrowed and she can't remember where to put her hands and feet, and her photographs are long forgotten.

But she would never call the sound mournful.

He doesn't ask her to promise she will see him again. Why pretend that is even possible now?

They share one of her cigarettes before going their separate ways.

W hat took so long?" asks her husband before she can put down her keys. Her hands still carry the scent of the afternoon.

He follows her into the kitchen, leans against the counter as she washes her hands.

"So, is the judge releasing your names?"

She turns off the spigots.

"She hasn't ruled."

"Why were you summoned, then?"

"She wanted to know what concerns we had about our names being released," she says, surprised at how easily she can lie.

"Please tell me no one wanted their names released."

"I don't know. We were interviewed individually in chambers."

"What did you say to the judge?"

"I said I wanted my life back."

Is this guilt she feels? She doesn't think so. Shame? It feels nothing like shame. She thinks it might be love in its most unstable state, but she doesn't know for whom that love is being summoned—her husband, who is now standing behind her, massaging her neck as she dries her hands, or the man holding his cat in the kitchen window.

That night, while her husband sleeps, Hannah enters her studio, a perfect cube facing the lake. One wall is glass, the other three are white and bare. Not even a pushpin remains of the failed series she had been working on for the past six months. The week before jury duty had started, she took down the photographs and deleted the images from her computer. The series had finally revealed itself for what it was—derivative. Not of some other photographer's work, but of her own, younger self.

When she still used a darkroom, and negatives, and an enlarger, and developer, and stop bath, and scissors, and fixer, the ritual of destroying failed projects had more pageantry. She could tear down the prints hanging by clothespins, crumple them up, stomp on the negatives or slam open the darkroom door to let daylight erase her work, rather than coldly press Delete.

Her husband salvaged more than one roll of film after she threatened to burn it in melodramatic doubt. A younger man, a man her own age, might have let her burn her negatives to teach her a lesson, might have been jealous of a melodrama from which he was excluded. Her husband merely waited for the tempest to pass and returned the untouched rolls of film the next morning.

It is just before dawn. Pink vapors are coming off the lake. The water is warmer than the air. She opens the slider for a moment. The insects and frogs are louder than New York traffic, the music of her youth.

. . .

Her husband lingers over his coffee after breakfast the next morning, the local paper open next to his elbow on the kitchen table.

As she reaches for the milk, she skims the stories above the fold.

WILL FREE LOVE LEAD TO FREEDOM?: ANCA BUTLER'S ATTORNEY WANTS A NEW TRIAL ON THE CLAIM THAT JURORS HAD SEX.

She knows by his incredulous yet titillated expression that he is reading the story. She retrieves her empty hand, the milk carton forgotten.

"Did you know?" he asks.

He takes her silence for a yes.

"Which jurors?"

When she doesn't answer again, he guesses: "The anatomy professor and the schoolteacher, the one you called 'hot date.'"

When she doesn't concur with his guess, he lobs another possibility. "The anatomy professor and the chemical engineer."

"Why are you so sure it was a man and a woman?"

It takes all her control and strength to maintain her light, gossipy smirk as she reads the story for herself. That smirk weighs a thousand pounds.

"The schoolteacher and the chemical engineer?"

"Why not Cornrows and the church lady?"

"You're not going to tell me, are you?"

"I'm under oath."

"You know you can't keep secrets from me." He pours himself a fresh coffee. "Cornrows and the alternate?"

Her husband's gift as a journalist had been his canny ability to suss out secrets from diplomats and generals. His editors thought he had a special talent, but Hannah knew it was just unrelenting persistence.

At lunch, he says, "Vegas odds agree with me, six to one, the schoolteacher and the anatomy professor."

Having grown up in Vegas, Hannah knows that book is made on anything: the length of the last note of Lady Gaga's "Star-Spangled Banner"—"BRAAAAVE"—during the Super Bowl, whether or not any of the Kardashians will appear at O.J.'s parole hearing, where space station Skylab's wreckage will fall to Earth.

"Did you bet?" she asks.

"Of course not. Don't you want to know what your odds are?"

"Don't you have a memoir to write?"

. . .

She is in a cell where the lights never go out and a white-noise machine is cranked up full volume and every time merciful sleep catches up to her, a bucket of ice water is thrown over her naked body. That's what waiting for her husband's next interrogation feels like.

. . .

Next morning, forbidden to publish the jurors' names, only their letters and numbers, the *Sentinel* profiles the six with facts gleaned from the *voir dire.*

Her husband reads aloud, " 'C-2 is a middle-aged married woman who moved to Alachua County ten years ago. She is a photographer. She had no prior knowledge of the case. She swims for recreation. During the *voir dire,* when asked why she married her husband, her answer was "To save money on taxes." ' "

"Did you really say that?"

"Because it's true."

He continues reading: " 'B-7 is a young single woman who grew up in Williston, Florida, and teaches middle school. She heard about the case in church. She is a pet lover. She enjoys salsa dancing.'

"Salsa dancing?" he says. "I bet that ups the odds."

After dinner, he watches cable news in the living room, while she remains in the kitchen reading F-17's profile. It tells nothing she doesn't already know, yet she reads it twice before texting him.

did you see the sentinel?

She waits while he reads the article on his phone.

it's unconscionable, but it's irrelevant.

vegas is already making book on which jurors had the affair, she types.

"Get in here. B-7 is on CNN," her husband calls.

the schoolteacher is on tv, she informs Graham, then hurries to the living room.

Dressed in baggy, androgynous clothes, her face pixilated, her voice intentionally distorted, she speaks with garbled urgency. She says she never had sex with another juror. Her life has been ruined. She will have to take a leave from her job and move out of the state. She says that now that professions have been leaked, the media should take a look at the anatomy professor and the photographer.

Her husband is never still: his feet tap, he scratches his arm, he examines his scalp, he cleans his fingernails, he wipes his glasses, he picks at the armrest. Stillness is antithetical to the atoms that give him energy. Yet he is still now. He looks at her as if he doesn't recognize her. His face tightens with rage, then abruptly loosens in anguish. At sixty, he might have punched a wall. At seventy, he might have punished her with silence. But at eighty-six, he sits back to catch his breath.

"Do you love him?"

"No." She begins her confession with a certainty she isn't certain of. The apology comes next, but he doesn't want to hear it.

"Let me talk! Are you going to keep seeing him?"

"It's over."

"Maybe for you. For me, it's just beginning."

He stands up too quickly, falters, gropes for the sofa's armrest, waits for the blood to return to his head. His breath quickens.

"Are you okay?" she asks cautiously.

"How could I be okay?"

He sinks down again, as if he realizes he has nowhere to go.

"Why?" he asks.

She tells him the truth as she understands it, which isn't much. "I wanted a last dalliance before I got too old."

"You couldn't wait until I'm dead?"

His feet tap, he scratches his arm, rubs his cheeks.

"Everyone knows," he says.

"Our names haven't been released."

"Yet."

He grabs his phone, pokes the screen with his unsteady index finger.

"What are you doing?" she asks.

"Shut up!"

He turns the screen around. The site is *Vegas*INSIDER.com.

"The odds have already turned in your favor," he says.

He picks at the armrest, examines his scalp.

"I want you to leave."

"May I pack a few things first?"

"Where are you going?"

"To a motel."

"Not to him?"

"It's over," she repeats.

As she opens the front door to leave, he says, "You can sleep in your studio tonight."

She arranges clean sheets on her daybed. Even though the studio door is shut, his pain and hurt waft under the jamb, like gas, and choke her. She is tempted to return to their bedroom to assure him, once again, that it's over, but she suspects the repetition of that assurance will have the opposite effect.

Around midnight, after the lights around the house go out, she slips back into the kitchen for food. She hasn't eaten since breakfast. As she opens the fridge, she spies her husband in the arctic gloom, seated at the kitchen table. He doesn't react to the sudden light. The stillness he now occupies is of a very different order than the afternoon's. The stillness is no longer suppressed anxiousness. This stillness is closer to hardened wax.

She sits across from him. His eyes are closed, as if he is listening to something very faint. He doesn't acknowledge her presence. She waits patiently and then not so patiently. "Are you okay?" she says at last.

"My heart keeps skipping a beat. I think something's wrong with my pacemaker. It's supposed to give off a beep when the battery runs low. Could you listen?"

She leans her ear against his barrel chest, against his skin. His heartbeat sounds like a faint but steady hammering on a pipe in a sunken ship at the bottom of the ocean, a signal to the outside world that someone is still alive.

"I don't hear any beeping," she says.

The look he gives her is harsher than accusation, blame, jealousy, wrath. The look is distrust. He doesn't believe her answer.

She retrieves her laptop from the studio. They listen to an online audio recording of a pacemaker's alarm just to be sure. When the battery is low, the sound resembles a distant truck backing up. When the battery is about to die, the sound becomes more urgent and resembles the siren the Nazis blared on their way to arrest Jews.

She listens again, ear to skin. Her husband had rickets as a child, and his fourth rib, deformed by lack of vitamin D, jabs against her temple like a club.

"The battery is fine," she says.

Without asking permission, she returns with him to their bed. She positions herself on the narrowest margin of mattress. He doesn't object.

"You'll wake me if your heart starts skipping?"

He doesn't acknowledge her, but she knows he will.

He is gone when she wakes up the next morning. When he returns around noon, he says, "If you're staying out of pity for an old man, you can leave now. The cardiologist just told me my heart is as strong as a man half my age."

"That's wonderful."

"Because you can leave without guilt?"

He sits on the sofa, stands, sits, half rises, then sinks again, this time for the count of ten.

"I know what living with an old man is costing you," he says. His voice has lost its biblical rage. She has to lean close to hear what he says next. "It's only going to get harder. Maybe you *should* leave? I'm scared."

When she reaches for his hand, he jerks it back. "How could you do this to me?"

.   .   .

She hears him on the phone with Lenny. His study door is shut, but the door is hollow. She can make out an occasional word. He must be telling his old friend about her betrayal. She hears her name. Her husband is silent for a long time after that. Lenny must be consoling him, or maybe men only advise? Can Lenny sincerely say "You'll get through this" to an eighty-six-year-old man? Or maybe that's exactly what Lenny is saying: "Your heart is as strong as a man half your age, you'll get through this."

When her husband comes out of his study, he looks as if he has endured a bloodletting. He touches the wall to steady himself. She follows him into the bedroom, uninvited.

"Is it your heart again?" she asks.

Without looking at her, he says, "The judge is going ahead with sentencing next Monday, after which she will release your names."

"Lenny said that?"

"Get out. I need to prepare myself," he says.

What does returning to bed at eleven o'clock in the morning prepare you for? Though she hasn't yet phrased the question aloud, he says, "Public humiliation."

She sits on the edge of the bed, uninvited.

"Please leave me alone," he says.

Before she reaches the door, he says, "I can't catch my breath."

She returns to his side. He allows her to rub his back. She takes the risk and holds him. He stiffens but doesn't object.

"Take deep breaths," she says. "You're having an anxiety attack."

"You aren't?"

He inhales and exhales deeply, as if he is blowing up a balloon.

Should she console him? *Your heart is as strong as a man half your age, you'll get through it.*

"We'll get through this," she says.

They make love for the first time since her return, almost a month ago. Her husband's need to prove to himself that his heart is as strong as a man half his age is greater than his need for her. His erection acts as a barometer of his moods. She can feel him soften. She doubts he reached a climax, but it hardly matters. The deed is done. *All happy marriages have sex; all unhappy marriages don't.*

.   .   .

As he walks naked to the bathroom the next morning, Hannah notices that the left side of his rib cage is bruised, as if they had wrestled last night rather than had sex. When he sees himself in the medicine cabinet mirror, he asks, "Did you hit me?"

"Why would you ask that?" she says, though she herself is wondering the same thing—was there a moment during sex when things got rough?

He stands in the doorway, his robe still hanging from a peg. He is getting shorter every day. His vertebrae are eroding. The rest of him, especially his torso and the organs within, have had to compact themselves into a smaller space with a lower ceiling. How do they all fit? Acting more like a basket than a cage, the ribs almost touch his hips. It would have been unthinkable to have rough sex with such frailty.

"I must have bumped myself. Did you notice it last night?" he asks.

The size of a fist, the bruise covers his clavicle down to the fourth rib, the club. She hadn't noticed it, but then again, her eyes had been closed. It is hard to make love to all that fragility with your eyes open.

"Should you have a doctor look at it?" she asks.

"Which one? Leavitt?"

"I don't know your doctors' names."

"My blood guy. Or should I just drive over to one of those twenty-four-hour doc-in-a-boxes?"

"I don't think it's an emergency."

Later, she hears him on the phone. He is telling the listener—his hematologist's nurse—about the bruise on his chest, and another bruise he didn't mention to Hannah, on his hip last week.

"Why didn't you mention the bruise on your hip?" she asks after he hangs up.

"I had other things on my mind."

. . .

Late Friday afternoon, a letter arrives from the court. Her husband answers the door, waits impatiently as Hannah opens the envelope.

The jurors' names will be released Monday, as Lenny had warned them. Hannah reads, "The court will do its utmost to protect you, our citizen-soldiers, who have done your duty and have been discharged. Media, or anyone else, attempting to contact the jury after the release of jurors' identities will be in contempt of court. Jurors who wish to discuss their service with the media are free to volunteer to do so at a press conference following the sentencing. The court will not allow this jury to be subjected to further intrusions into their private lives."

Whatever intimacy was rekindled during sex is immediately doused. His posture, which had slowly been straightening as he got his footing again, collapses. With a shortened spine, the collapse is far more angled than crumbling, a balancing rock that shifts but doesn't fall. His chin juts out, one shoulder rises, the other slopes, and a small ridge forms on his back.

"Are you going to speak at the press conference?" he asks.

A response isn't necessary. "Do you want to go away, somewhere, just get on a plane?"

"Alone?"

Once the boulder slips, it can't be re-righted.

"Together," she says.

"I don't know if I can go anywhere with you."

That night, she wakes to the sensation of being trapped under an avalanche with a hot engine. She reaches across the bed, keeping her hand above his brow so as not to wake him. The heat is emanating from his skin. The sheets around him are damp from sweat.

Can someone have a panic attack in their sleep?

Angling her tablet's bright screen so as not to disturb him, she reads, *Nocturnal panic attacks include rapid heart rate, trembling, shortness of breath, hyperventilation, flushing or chills, sweats. People perspire when they fear danger so that the body's water can be eliminated through the skin rather than through the kidneys—so that you don't have to stop to urinate in the midst of defending yourself from danger or escaping harm.*

Even in a dream?

In a nightmare.

Sunday morning, he announces his plans. After he sees his blood guy, he is leaving the country. He doesn't say where. For the remainder of the day, he doesn't behave like a man preparing for a long trip. He looks more like a man preparing for an enormous wave to drag him to the bottom of the ocean without a pipe to hammer on for help.

.   .   .

Hannah sits in the living room on Monday morning watching the courthouse's plaza in real time on her tablet, courtesy of a website she found over the weekend, AbovetheLaw.org. Her husband is in his study, though she doubts he is playing Solitaire.

The protestors are back, but the webcam isn't angled in their favor. A picket sign is occasionally thrust into view but too fast to read.

At ten sharp, the courthouse doors open. The first reporter out is the university alum who aspires to be a crime reporter. Youthful and fit, she sprints across the plaza to her cameraman, and begins talking without any sign that she just did a hundred-yard dash in under fifteen seconds. Next out, the middle-aged CNN reporter, not as fit, and looking as if he has opened an oven door. His shirt darkens with sweat. He stands close enough to the webcam for the microphone to pick up his voice.

Anca has been sentenced to fourteen years, the first two of which will be served in a juvenile facility.

The webcam suddenly goes dead, which doesn't trouble Hannah. She is not interested in the hoopla that follows the sentencing. She is waiting for the press conference arranged for any juror who wants their fifteen minutes in the limelight.

The webcam goes live again. It is now set up in the room where the original pool of potential jurors waited for their numbers to be called. A bouquet of microphones is set up in front. Minutes pass and no one comes forward.

Then the alternate approaches the microphones. He asks the audience if everyone can hear him. He introduces the man with him as his lawyer and agent. He says he hasn't prepared a statement but will take questions.

"*Us Weekly*," a reporter introduces himself. "Did the whole jury know about the affair, and do you believe the jury was able to reach an impartial verdict under the circumstances?"

The alternate shields his lips, whispers something to his lawyer and agent. Hannah guesses that he doesn't know what "impartial" means.

If he wants to sell his story to the tabloids, he will have to shoe-horn himself into it. "I was the one who caught her going into his room in the middle of the night. I was getting ice. She pretended she had the wrong room. I didn't say anything, because I was only an alternate at that point."

"The *Orlando Sentinel*," another reporter introduces herself. "How did the jury divide over the question of guilt?"

"We all voted guilty on the first round except for . . . am I allowed to say names? We all thought Hannah only voted not guilty to get back at Doc—we called him Doc—because he dumped her."

She turns off the tablet, sets it facedown on the armrest, and heads to her husband's study to see if he has been watching too. He isn't there. The screen is frozen on a game of Solitaire. He won.

She finds him in the bedroom, putting on his shoes, collecting his keys.

"I'm seeing Leavitt at ten. There was a cancellation."

"I want to go with you."

He looks at her as if she is glare itself. "Your name was just released. Do you mind if I don't want my doctor's appointment turned into your soap opera?"

"I'll wait in the car."

"It never occurred to you that it would end like this?"

His fury has returned, but it is no longer biblical. It is Talmudic. He guns the Prius, as if the silent electric car can muster rage, before fishtailing away.

. . .

did you watch the press conference? she texts Graham.

did you go? he texts back.

Her phone vibrates with an incoming call, a number she doesn't recognize.

a reporter is calling, she texts.

don't answer.

Another tremor from an unknown caller.

write down the number, he texts. *alert the court. the judge ruled reporters were not allowed to contact us.*

She can see by the three lights flashing in Graham's thought bubble that he has more to say.

I wish I could see you.

The incoming calls don't stop. The count by the voicemail icon is now at nine. On the tenth ring, her husband's name appears.

"Hy?" she answers.

"You speak to her," she hears her husband tell someone.

"This is Dr. Leavitt," says a concerned male voice. "My nurse has been trying to reach you. I'm afraid the news isn't good. Your husband has leukemia."

"Tell her the prognosis," she hears her husband say in the background.

"Your husband wants me to tell you the prognosis," says the doctor. His elocution of the word "prognosis" is so much more grounded than her husband's anguished version.

"If we give him transfusions, and if he can tolerate the transfusions, maybe months."

"And if he can't tolerate them?" Hannah asks.

"Weeks."

"Are there no other treatments?"

"We could do a bone-marrow biopsy."

"And what would that tell us?"

"Whether he has weeks or months."

"There's nothing experimental, a trial?"

"Not at his age."

Is her husband sitting right there, listening?

"May I talk to him?"

"Hello, who is this?" asks her husband.

"Me."

"Did you talk to the doctor?"

"Yes."

"Did he tell you the prognosis?" This time his pronunciation of the word "prognosis" is closer to the doctor's, if the word "grounded" included planets other than Earth.

.   .   .

He is asleep in the crowded waiting area on a chair under a television tuned to the HGTV channel when she arrives. His blood guy practices in the hematology department of the university's medical center, a vast complex of buildings connected by underground tunnels, like termite hills.

Under the hammering and sawing on the television where a renovation is under way, her husband, head back, mouth open, looks more unconscious than asleep.

She should have insisted on going with him. There had been no need to worry about her infamy here. Among the souls hunkered in wheelchairs and attached to drips, her soap opera is but a stepped-on anthill.

She kneels before him and puts her head on his lap. "I'm sorry you had to hear this alone," she says.

The arm that wears a cotton ball with a dollop of blood in the crux of the elbow stirs. He takes her hand.

"I'm so discouraged," he says.

"The doctor told me that with transfusions, you could have months."

"Only months?"

"You ready to get out of here?" she asks in her bravest voice, neither contralto nor mezzo-soprano, but tinny.

He slumps into the wheelchair that the nurse provides to help Hannah navigate him to the Prius. He thinks he remembers that he parked the car in the first of four concrete towers, or maybe it was the second tower? She pushes him up and down ramps. She can't tell if pushing uphill is harder than braking downhill. The medical center's parking lot should provide emergency lanes for runaway wheelchairs, like steep highways do for runaway trucks. Just as she is about to give up and call a cab, she presses the Unlock button on her key fob one last time, and the Prius calls back to them.

He sleeps all the way home. She struggles to get him into bed. She draws all the blinds, in case reporters are lurking about undeterred by the judge's ruling. She unplugs the landline, powers off her cell and his. Finally, she has a chance to sit down, collect herself, and take a moment to listen to the crushing silence.

Her husband sleeps all afternoon and evening. Even so, she waits until his normal bedtime before she emails Graham. She needs a second opinion, and he is the only doctor she knows who will read her email after midnight.

She lists everything the doctor told her and all her husband's stats and counts and tests. She provides Graham with the username and password of her husband's medical records, so he can see past test results and judge the progress of the disease. She types, *Do you agree with the prognosis?*

"Has something else happened?" her husband asks, standing in her studio doorway. He looks like himself, as he was this morning, before he left for the doctor, like a man who has years.

"I'm on a website where you can get a second opinion," she says, pressing Send.

He sits on the chair purchased from IKEA more than twenty-six years ago.

"Dr. Leavitt called it 'galloping' cancer," he says.

"What an awful term."

"I always thought I would die in my sleep, just not wake up one day."

"That's because you're an optimist," Hannah says.

"Will you finish my memoir?"

She can't tell if he is serious. "Isn't a memoir an act of memory," she says.

"I've reached the years after you came into my life. You know what happens."

"Yes," she promises him, though she knows she will file the memoir away unfinished, in a box she will later send to the university to join his other papers in the archives, a warren of vaults under the library.

As soon as her husband falls asleep again, she returns to her studio to see if Graham has answered her. Tens of emails, with usernames like AncaEyelashes, fill her inbox. The subject lines read: "Yes, now we know who the stupidest people in the world are," "I know where you live."

Finally, she finds Graham's answer.

Yes, I agree with the prognosis.

. . .

The studio's glass wall, especially at night, always makes her feel like prey, as if an owl could swoop in and grab her by her hair. She douses the lights. It is so dark in the woods by the lake. Is someone out there, a reporter willing to break the court order, or is it Death coming for her husband?

As she enters their bedroom, she hears him crying. He is wracked in sobs, wracked as in that instrument of torture—the medieval rack.

She gives him his privacy until the sobs subside. He has every right to cry for what is about to be taken from him. Everything.

When she finally returns to bed, he says, "It's hard to believe that I'm not going to be here in a few weeks."

She crosses the mattress to hold him. The mattress is made of a space-age sponge that conforms to the body. She sinks into the hollow he has made for himself.

"You could have months," she says.

"It's just as impossible to accept that I'm not going to be here in a few months," he says.

She can't think of a response, because there is none.

"Distract me, please," he says.

"You want me to read to you?"

"I want you to talk to me."

"Anything?"

"I just need to hear your voice."

Her husband has always distracted himself with legal thrillers.

"Would you like to know why I thought Anca was guilty?"

"Yes."

She begins with the evidence, but evidence—burned as opposed to singed eyelashes, paint thinner as opposed to gasoline—isn't distracting enough for a man who has only weeks to live.

She changes her strategy. She describes Anca's expressionless sketchbook face, the far prettier twin sister, the incremental turning of Anca's head, the affectless confession, and the chocolate bars consumed during closing arguments.

"She displayed emotion only once during the entire trial. When her twin sister testified about the time Anca's dachshund ate a sago nut and died," Hannah tells him.

All her husband says in response is "Did the dog suffer?"

In a curtained room, a nurse offers her husband the choice of either a hospital bed or an armchair to use while he undergoes the transfusion. His full weight is on Hannah's arm. Over the past twenty-four hours his decline has been just as Dr. Leavitt said: galloping. He chooses the chair even though Hannah knows he wants the bed, because choosing the bed would be giving in.

The nurse returns with the blood cart, enough bags of blood for a horror film.

"Is this all for me?" her husband asks.

"We'll start with one," the nurse says.

Hannah needs a cigarette. "I'm going for a cup of coffee," she tells her husband. "You want one?"

"Am I allowed to drink?" he asks the nurse.

"As long as it's not alcohol," the nurse says, hanging a bag of blood from a hook over the chair in which her husband fidgets. The stiff vinyl armchair is to a normal armchair what a pair of diabetic shoes is to Italian loafers.

Hannah leaves the hospital and searches for a place to smoke. She doesn't care that the university forbids smoking. Let them arrest her. She joins two other rebels who are puffing away near the ambulance bay. The volume of patients funneling into the medical center looks like a pilgrimage to Lourdes. She knows Graham works nearby. She can't help but look for him. She doesn't necessarily want to speak to him, just to see him. This yearning isn't going to end anytime soon.

A woman, tugging her toddler by the wrist, approaches Hannah. "I hope you drown!" she says, scooping the child up and striding away.

Hannah isn't sure if the fury was directed at her cigarette or the verdict. Why did she say "drown"? Did she read C-2's profile in the *Sentinel*? *Swims for recreation.*

She crushes out her cigarette and returns to the man tethered to the bag of blood.

"You forgot my coffee," he says when he notices that she is empty-handed.

"I'm sorry," she says. "You still want one?"

"Never mind, Dr. Death wants to talk to us about my wishes."

Is he hallucinating? Is she?

"Who is Dr. Death?"

"I overheard the nurses call him that. Nice guy. His specialty is palliative care. He wants me to sign a DNR. I told him no."

The bag of blood doesn't appear to be any emptier than when she left.

A young slender Indian man steps through the curtain.

"This is the doctor I was telling you about. My wife, Mrs. Richler."

It takes Hannah a second to realize that her husband is referring to her. She never took his name. Mrs. Richler is what she calls her husband's former wives.

"Mrs. Richler," the doctor says, "I told your husband earlier that it was entirely up to him whether or not he wants to be resuscitated if his heart stops."

Her husband pulls at the blanket, bites a cuticle.

She kneels before him. "You want the doctors to try everything?" she asks.

He removes his glasses, cleans them with the hospital sheet. He still doesn't entirely trust her, but what choice does he have.

"If there's hope," he says at last.

"He's not going to sign," she tells the doctor.

"What happens to me after my heart is resuscitated?" her husband asks.

"We would probably have to induce a coma for both the pain and the intubation."

"The pain?"

"At your age, bones break easily. Most likely, many of your ribs will be fractured from the chest compressions."

"Where do I sign?"

Hannah is given a wallet-size version of the signed DNR to keep on her at all times.

The bag takes three more hours to empty. The nurse comes in with a second bag.

"Enough," her husband says.

.   .   .

In the parking garage, wheeling her husband to the car, she again has that sense of being prey. Someone *is* stalking her. She reels around, strides toward the pillar where she is positive she saw the glint of a lens.

An overweight man, puddled in sweat, and necklaced by telephonic lenses, hides as best he can.

What could she possibly yell at him that he hasn't heard before?

"Enough!" she yells.

By the time she gets back to her husband, the wheelchair has drifted downhill. Her husband is braking with his outstretched sandaled feet. She catches him just before the curve.

"How could you leave me alone?" he asks.

Feet planted on the floor, he is half off the bed, half on, the posture of a man who has passed out from a night of hard drinking, but the scene lacks all the joys of inebriation. Only a drunken old poet would imagine that he is going to rage against the dying of the light. At whom? Death is excessively attentive. Death taps her husband's shoulder each time he falls asleep, startling him awake only long enough to remember that he is going to die. Death puts ice packs on his already cold feet. Death fills his bladder so that if he should stay asleep and forget that he is going to die, urgency reminds him.

She covers him with a blanket.

"Did the doctor call?" he asks without opening his eyes.

"Were you expecting him to?"

"He should have the blood test results by now, see if the transfusion worked."

"I can look up the test results online."

"We won't know what the numbers mean."

"I can get an answer from that second-opinion site I told you about."

. . .

Graham confirms what she already knows: the transfusion hasn't had much of an impact on the numbers.

She sits on the bed's edge next to her husband, but she doesn't touch him. He screamed out in pain the last time she hugged him.

"I already know," he says. "It didn't work."

She tells him that she would give him ten years from the remainder of her life if she could.

"I would never accept them," he says.

"We have a decision to make," she says. "When the time comes, do you want to go to the hospital or stay at home?"

He looks at her as if he has forgotten that he is going to die, and she just reminded him.

"Here or the hospital?" she repeats.

"Here?"

"Here?"

"Here," he says.

.   .   .

The hospice nurse is a large Jamaican woman with a buck-up joviality that Hannah can see her husband trusts. She opens the drapes, which haven't been opened since the release of Hannah's identity.

"We prefer them closed," Hannah tells her.

The nurse examines her husband, who is now sitting up in bed.

"Aren't you going to take my blood pressure?" he asks.

"You don't need to worry about your blood pressure any longer," the nurse says.

"I don't have to take my pills?"

Hannah can see that her husband is gobsmacked by the finality of not having to worry about his blood pressure.

"What about my pain pills?" he asks.

"We have better ones," the nurse says. "Do you like ice cream?"

"Who doesn't?" he says.

"You can now eat as much ice cream as you want."

The nurse helps her husband undress for a sponge bath. His exposed skin looks so white against her black hands. Black and white, the only two colors photographers had to work with for the camera's first hundred years.

Before leaving, after promising she will return tomorrow, the nurse hands Hannah a booklet, *When the Time Comes.* The photograph on the cover is a leaf floating on water. Hannah only allows herself a glance at the table of contents.

Goals at the End of Life
Withdrawal
Changes in Eating
Changes in Toileting
Changes in Breathing
Changes in Body Temperature
Confusion
Restlessness and Anxiety
Vision-like Experiences
Wave of Energy
Saying Goodbye
When Death Is Near
Moment of Death

A fever consumes her husband one night. In his delirium, he throws off the blankets, peels away his T-shirt. Hannah can see that all the bruises on his back and buttocks have connected. They are no longer islands.

After she explains to the hospice nurse on call that her husband is feverish and a continent of bruises has taken over his body, the nurse instructs, "Take his temperature."

The number is just shy of one hundred and two.

"Give him two Tylenols," the nurse instructs, "then take his temperature again in a half hour, and call back with the results."

At the half-hour mark, the results baffle Hannah. Her husband has gone cold.

"He's shivering," she tells the nurse.

His teeth are chattering so violently that he gives himself a nosebleed.

"He's hemorrhaging."

"Have him sit up and tilt his head forward. Pinch the soft part of his nose shut. If the bleeding doesn't stop in the next fifteen minutes, call me," the nurse says.

Pinching his nostrils doesn't stop it. Tissues don't dam it. The face towel is useless.

Only five minutes have passed. How much blood can he lose?

She calls Graham: "All the blood that was dripped into him four days ago is gushing out. What should I do?"

"Do you want me to come over?"

"He'll recognize you."

"He never met me."

"Who will we tell him you are?"

"The night nurse."

· · ·

The bleeding has subsided to a manageable drip by the time Graham arrives. Hannah stops him at the front door to tell him that the emergency is over and to turn him away. She almost feels as if she should provide proof that the emergency was real—the wadded red tissues—and that she didn't betray her husband for nothing.

"Have the night nurse come in, he's here anyway," her husband calls from his hospital bed in the living room.

Graham asks her husband to continue pinching his nose while he examines the bruises on his back, listens to his heart. The image is so teethed with irony that even if Hannah had her camera, she wouldn't take a picture.

Yes she would.

He reaches for her husband's arm to slip a cuff above the elbow and pump air into its pressurized sleeve. Her husband's muscles have shrunk from ropes to strings. She wants to tell Graham that her husband was once a mass of energy, a gravitational force that drew worlds to him—not the skeleton whose blood pressure Graham is taking.

"The daytime nurse never takes my blood pressure," her husband says.

"I can stop if you want."

"No," her husband says. "What's my blood pressure?"

Graham glances at Hannah for her permission to toll the death bell. Her husband's numbers are shockingly low, the numbers you might read on a bicycle pump when the tire is nearly flat.

"What is happening to me?" her husband asks.

When Graham again studies Hannah to verify her permission, her husband says, "Don't look at her. I have a right to know."

"You're in circulatory failure."

"What does that mean?"

"You're dying."

"Now?"

"You have days, not weeks."

It has begun, Hannah thinks. Can you say "It has begun" about the end?

She walks Graham to his car to thank him, but all she wants is to get back to her husband.

"I don't want to put us through this any longer," her husband says when she sits on the edge of his hospital bed, positioned in the living room so that he can see the lake at all times, if he can keep his eyes open.

"I'm only going to get worse," he says.

His voice has returned to its former confidence.

"If I was your old dog, tomorrow is the day you would put me to sleep."

"Let's see how you feel in the morning," she says, though that makes no sense to a man who has days.

"If I was your old dog," he tells the daytime nurse when she asks him to rank his pain on a scale between one and ten, "today is the day you would put me down."

This time he says "down," not "to sleep."

"Only if my dog was ready," the nurse says.

"I'm ready," her husband says.

I n muffled hysteria, concealed behind a mask as expressionless as Anca's, Hannah watches as the nurse lines up three different pill vials, liquid morphine, ten oral syringes, and eye drops.

"The prescription says to take .5 milligrams by mouth every two hours as needed for pain and distress." She fills one of the oral syringes all the way up to the top, ignoring the halfway point indicated in the directions. Then she fills a second syringe. "I find it is better to have two or three syringes prepared beforehand. Hands get shaky. Why don't you try filling one yourself?"

Hannah inserts the plastic nose into the tea-colored liquid, pulls back the stopper. When the fluid reaches .5 milligrams, she looks over at the nurse, whose return stare remains completely neutral, almost beatific. Hannah fills the syringe.

"The bottle says to administer every two hours, but it also says 'as needed for pain and distress,'" the nurse says, handing Hannah another syringe. "If your husband is in pain and distress, I would give him the medicine every hour, maybe every half hour."

There are now four full syringes on the kitchen counter.

"You know, if you want, you can fill all ten syringes," the nurse says. She waits for Hannah to acknowledge her subtext. When Hannah nods enigmatically, the nurse repeats, "Do you understand?"

"What if I run out of morphine?" Hannah asks.

"Why don't I have the doctor call in a second prescription, just in case you accidentally spill this one."

The nurse reaches for the first vial and shakes out three tiny white pills. "Alprazolam. For anxiety. Sometimes patients get very restless. This will calm him." She picks up the second vial, also little white pills. "Hyoscine butylbromide. It helps with secretion."

Secretion?

"Give it to him with the alprazolam," the nurse instructs. She uncaps the third vial. "Haloperidol, for delirium. Just in case."

She takes two teaspoons and crushes the pills into powder. "Extend his lower lip and put the powder between the lip and gums."

She holds up the eye drops. "For nausea. If he can't open his eyes, gently pull back his lid and give him .3 milligrams."

Hannah can only imagine what it will be like to open her husband's lid, and see the fear underneath, or, worse, the absence of fear. Her kitchen table now resembles a hospital cart. "What if I make a mistake?" she asks the nurse.

"There are no mistakes," the nurse says.

. . .

Her husband is alert when Hannah returns from walking the nurse out.

"I feel better than I have in days," he says, sitting himself up with the help of the bed's hydraulics. "Maybe the transfusion is working?"

Hannah read the chapter *Wave of Energy* in the hospice booklet: *The dying may experience a sudden burst of energy. It is easy to see how this can give false hope that the patient is getting better. The patient may be building up strength for the last full-body moment in this life.*

"I think I'm hungry," her husband says.

By the time Hannah returns with a tray of possibilities—cookies, crackers, yogurt, ice cream—he has fallen unconscious again. She can no longer call the state he occupies "sleep." She can almost sense the energy as it evaporates off his skin.

Is he ready? Is she? Does she wake him up to ask permission again, just to be sure? *Do you still want to die?* Who would want to be asked that? Shouldn't his last memory be of appetite, of hope? *If there is still hope,* he had told Dr. Death.

She gives him one full syringe of morphine, between his gum and his lip, as the nurse instructed. Twice the amount prescribed, but not lethal. While his mouth is still open, she dusts his gums with the pulverized pills, spilling powder on his chin.

Is he already moving through the tunnel toward the white light? Is he about to be greeted by dead loved ones? Neurologists ascribe the experience to a flood of dopamine. What if such an ecstasy of chemistry exists and the morphine robs him of that final pleasure?

She opens his lid to administer the eye drops. What she sees isn't ecstasy. His pupil eclipses the watery brown iris, which appears to be seeping into the adjacent white. Is this what suffering looks like?

She gives him another dose of morphine, and then waits at his bedside for his presence to disperse into the universe.

She doesn't cry. The tears would only be for herself.

She reaches for the hospice booklet and reads the chapter *When Death Is Near.*

Below is a list of signs that may mean death will take place soon. Each person's dying process is unique. Keep in mind, this is only a basic guide.

Changes in skin color.
Long breaks between breaths.

Weak heartbeat.
Drop in blood pressure.
Less urine or no urine.
Eyelids don't close all the way.

She looks up at his eyes, which have opened.

"Are you there?" she asks.

She looks closer. His pupils have shrunk to pencil points.

At the two-hour mark, when the prescription allows for another .5 milligrams, she empties three syringes.

She helps herself to two of his tranquilizers, and stretches out on the sofa, within earshot of his rattled breathing. His gasps for air are now broken by longer periods of silence.

He is still alive when she wakes up five minutes or five hours later. She doesn't know.

She repeats the routine. Three doses of morphine. Three pulverized tranquilizers, two crushed hyoscine butylbromides, and a dollop of water. If she were on trial, couldn't the prosecutor make a good case for murder? The younger wife, the lover, the old husband. When the pills have completely dissolved, she rubs, as gently as possible, the paste between his gum and his lip. She opens the drapes so that her husband has a view of the lake. If the stalkarazzis are out there, let them take pictures.

This is anything but murder.

This is the bravest, kindest act she has ever done.

She reaches for the eye drops. His eyes have closed again, and she has to open a lid. The iris is now gone. It has floated away. She suddenly realizes that she hasn't heard a breath for some time. She presses her ear to his chest. The hammering from the sunken ship has stopped.

.   .   .

Her husband only observed one religious act, cherry-picked from his Orthodox Jewish upbringing: the lighting of the Yahrzeit candle on the anniversary of his mother's death. Hannah has read somewhere that Jews wash their dead loved ones as a form of respect and farewell.

Do you use a common washcloth?

She prepares a bowl of water with a dollop of liquid soap. There is no longer any reason to wait for the water to get warm.

As she washes the body, it no longer feels like her husband. He only abandoned it minutes ago, and it is already not him.

Did his memories exit with those last exhalations? His childhood. Gone. Their marriage. Gone. The deformed rib on which she rested her head already decaying.

After she finishes washing the body, she gets her camera. The unspoken bonus of their ridiculous age gap had been that her husband knew enough not to compete with her photography. He would have wanted her to take the memento mori. He would have encouraged her to be as merciless as need be for a good photograph. He would have reminded her of what she had told him: You either photograph what you know, or you photograph what you want to know. But the giants photograph what they don't want to know.

She aims the camera, but she doesn't click.

Does she need proof of what she is seeing? Couldn't she just blink, as she has been doing lately, record the image for her memory alone?

She blinks.

And blinks.

And blinks.

Not to take symbolic photographs, not to record, not to score the image on her brain, not to block out visual stimuli.

She blinks simply to fight back the tears.

Then she thinks, *Why fight?*

"Your prescription is ready," says an automated voice.

Hannah hangs up.

An hour later, the landline rings again: "Your prescription is ready."

She presses the only number on the menu that promises a human voice.

"Your prescription is ready," the pharmacist tells her after a ten-minute wait.

"For what?"

"Morphine."

"I no longer need it," Hannah says. "It's too late."

"You'll need to come in to sign a form saying you never picked it up. It's a Schedule II narcotic."

"My husband died twenty-four hours ago, and I must appear in person with a photo ID to stop the harassing calls."

"I'm sorry for your loss."

After a harrowing drive of her own making, she strides past the candies, the shampoos, the pet food, to the rear of the store, where four people ahead of her are waiting for the pharmacist. Shouldn't there be a separate line for the bereaved? Next to the register is the rack of tabloids. She drinks in the headlines, bracing herself for a mention of the trial, or, worse, the stalkarazzi's photograph of her screaming, *"ENOUGH!"* Or, worse still, a telephoto close-up, taken from the angle of the woods behind her house, of her killing her husband.

A new face, as pretty as Stephana's, now occupies the upper right-hand corner of *OK!* MURDER BY TEXT, the headline reads. "IT'S NOW OR NEVER," MICHELLE CARTER TEXTED HER SUICIDAL BOYFRIEND WHEN HE FLINCHED BEFORE TAKING HIS LIFE.

We're yesterday's news, Hannah tells her husband. She isn't talking to herself. Just because he is no longer here doesn't mean that their marriage has ended. "Till death do you part" is a suggestion, not an edict.

She taps her foot, scratches her arm, glances around. A man is buying hearing aid batteries, a woman is reading a vitamin label. Hannah's anonymity has been returned. No one is watching her.

Including her husband.

. . .

Grief doesn't feel as if a rug has been pulled out from under her. There is no rug. There is no floor on which to lay a rug. There is no ground on which to build a floor to lay a rug.

. . .

Lenny calls.

"Did he leave directives?" he asks when she tells him that she hasn't made any funeral arrangements.

Hannah vaguely remembers a file her husband once showed her, titled "Dementia or death." She opens the cabinet in her husband's study. The file contains all his passwords, copies of their wills, both monetary and living, a list of their bank accounts, his frequent flyer numbers, and a letter from the Anatomical Board of the State of Florida.

> *Dear Mr. Richler,*
>
> *We have received one copy of the properly executed form on which you dedicated your body to the Anatomical Board of the State of Florida for use in medical education.*
>
> *Please accept this letter as a very small demonstration of our gratitude and respect for your enormous generosity. You are to be commended for your broad-minded decision. It is our sincere hope, as we know it is yours, that such acts will contribute to the advancement of medical knowledge and thereby improve the quality of life for others.*

The letter is dated twelve years ago, when her husband first started teaching at the university, before he knew about the anatomy professor.

"He willed his body to science," she tells Lenny, then asks him, as her lawyer, to call the university and get her husband's body transferred to another medical school.

She doesn't explain her request. Lenny already knows about the anatomy professor.

He is quiet long enough for her to think the call was dropped.

"It's not your decision to make," Lenny says. "Last wish means exactly that, the very last hope someone had."

If there is still hope.

.   .   .

A dissection isn't only about how someone died, Graham had told her, it's about how someone lived. Her husband, who had recycled rubber bands and tin foil, wanted his body not to be wasted.

He will lie prone, only his back exposed, supposedly the least personal part of the body, but Hannah was skeptical when Graham first told her that, the night he demonstrated on her. Maybe the back is impersonal to a stranger, but Hannah knows her husband's back as intimately as she knows her own hand, the most personal part of the body, if she is to believe Graham.

Next, Graham, or one of his students, will roll her husband supine and make a series of lateral incisions, lifting off the rib cage, including the deformed rib. Graham will then explain to his students that the rib was deformed by a childhood case of rickets.

At some point, Graham will reach into her husband's chest, into the mediastinum, to unleash the veins and aortas from the posterior sac, and hold up the organ to demonstrate to the students how her husband's heart once beat.

She will never let those hands touch her again.

In days of the weeks that are indistinguishable to Hannah, the television remains on as a reminder that the world continues on the far side of the lake. Television voices are more comforting than music. Music makes Hannah feel. Music makes her want to dance.

The restlessness that had contributed to her ridding the house of all her husband's things—his suits, his shoes, his reading glasses, his lucky pebble, his hearing aids, his hearing aid batteries, his collection of Ace bandages, his electric toothbrush, his ointments, his compression socks, his inventory of vitamins in which he placed so much hope, the gallons of leftover Ensure—has been replaced by frenetic stasis. She doesn't suffer the panic of a trapped animal. The experience is closer to a person told to wait at a specific spot for someone who is late.

Who is she waiting for?

The only time her attention is able to assemble the world on the far side of the lake is when she reads or watches anything to do with the Anca Butler trial. Courtesy of YouTube, she has seen Anca's sentence hearing four times. While the sentencing is under way, Hannah is back in the courtroom, not here in the silent house.

"I would like to apologize to Mom and Dad for all this." Anca reads a handwritten statement on a folded piece of paper. "I only wanted to prove to you how much I loved Caleb. I still have no idea how this happened, and I really wish I did. I go to sleep every night and wake up every morning and wish I could change what happened."

Hannah doesn't believe that Anca wrote the note by herself. The word "prove" doesn't appear natural in the teenager's mumbled allocution. Who helped her write it? Her lawyer? Her mother? Her twin? The second paragraph is what interests Hannah.

"I destroyed two lives that day, Caleb's and my sister Stephana's. No one believes she is innocent. I want to say to my parents, and the court, that Stephana never told me to start the fire and she never told me to confess. My lawyer didn't want me to write this last line but it is true. I am a monster and I deserve to rot in jail."

To counter Anca's locking herself inside a cell and throwing away the key, her defense counsel calls character witnesses to the stand— Anca's teacher, Anca's maternal grandmother, Anca's former psychiatrist, and, finally, the parents.

The father goes first. He chokes out his words. He can barely suppress his rage. "I knew something was wrong the next day. We spent the night after the fire at my mother-in-law's. My wife and I took the sleeper sofa. When I woke up, Anca was standing over me. Usually when she would wake me up she would stand at the foot of the bed and shake my foot. But that morning she was standing by my waist, staring down at me and her mother . . . kind of creeped me out."

"Did she leave?" the defense counsel asks.

"Yeah, she walked out, said she needed to feed her dogs. We stuck them in my mother-in-law's garage."

"Did you see Anca any other time that day?"

"No. I think she stayed in the garage. I don't know. We were making funeral arrangements for my son."

"Would you say you and Anca are close?"

"She killed my son. I only want to talk about that. I only want to talk about Caleb."

The mother goes next. She tells the court that Anca was a quiet child who loved animals. The emotional contortions her features assume are too complex to register. Hannah is reminded of the animal faces she once captured at the moment when the animal realized that nothing more could be done for her offspring.

But Hannah isn't behind a camera now. There is no manipulating this next memory. She is standing over her husband with the last syringe of morphine. Before dosing him, she rests her head on his chest to listen to his life one last time before she takes it.

She becomes aware of the hearing again. The judge is pronouncing the sentence. Anca's features may look expressionless to the judge and the media, but Hannah can see the quiet child who loved animals. She still doesn't know what happened on the afternoon of the fire, and she will never know.

A letter arrives from Beverly—Cornrows—the last person on the jury who Hannah would have ever imagined writing to her. A belated condolence letter? They still trickle in after four months. Hannah normally throws them away unread. It isn't out of disrespect for the sender, quite the opposite. She imagines too deeply what he or she went through trying to articulate what is beyond language before finally resigning themselves to a string of clichés.

But the peculiarity of hearing from one of the jurors makes her open this one.

It isn't a condolence card, but an invitation to a reunion of the jurors to mark six months since the trial ended. The restaurant's location will remain secret until the last minute, in case the media gets wind of it. The invitation includes a letter from Beverly, who is organizing the reunion. The letter mentions "closure," a word antithetical to Hannah's lexicon, unless it is applied to physical wounds or men's flies.

Hannah has no intention of going.

On the way back to the house, she finds a dead raccoon by the pool. How did she not notice it on the way to the mailbox? It lies in a rocky drainage ditch by the fence. Giving it a wide berth, she circles the body, which to her shock opens its right eye. The eye orbits heavenward to take in the cloudless sky before noticing Hannah. The raccoon doesn't look rabid, it looks as bewildered by its own mortality as her husband was. In evident discomfort, the creature rolls onto its back, shuts its eyes. She knows it is close to death because she recognizes the signs from the hospice manual.

Long breaks between breaths.
Eyelids won't close all the way.

She phones Animal Control, then returns to the raccoon with a bowl of water and a bowl of potato chips. Setting the bowls down on the deck, she then pushes them closer with the pool skimmer.

The raccoon doesn't want food or water. It keeps switching positions, back to left side, left side to right side, sitting up, without any success in finding comfort.

Then, to Hannah's astonishment, the raccoon drags itself to the edge of the pool and slides in, headfirst. It swims in circles, almost joyous—*the dying may experience a sudden burst of energy*—until it can swim no longer. Using the skimmer and pole, Hannah helps it out of the pool.

They wait together for Animal Control.

The officer is a woman, wearing only garden gloves for protection.

"He won't eat," Hannah tells her as she removes a cage from the rear of the van.

Slumped against the fence, the raccoon is licking pool water from its lips.

"I wouldn't think so," the woman says.

After assessing the situation, she angles the cage so that the raccoon has nowhere else to go, and begins pushing the weak, bewildered animal inside with the handy pool skimmer.

"What will happen to him?" Hannah asks.

"He'll be euthanized, the poor creature."

After the van drives off with the dying raccoon, Hannah rereads Beverly's letter.

Save the date!!

Hello Fellow Jurors!!

I don't know about you all but I never in my lifetime thought I would experience something like it. We were all called to do our duty by the court and that is what we did. We each gave so much of ourselves during the trial. And after we did our duty, we were treated with hatred and lost our right to privacy. It is time we get together and have closure.

Had the raccoon not chosen to die by her pool, Hannah might not have gone.

. . .

She follows the Red Lobster hostess to a back room reserved for private parties.

Graham is already at the table, flanked by Beverly, who has gotten rid of her cornrows, and Amanda, the schoolteacher, who sports a new engagement ring. Hannah has only spoken to Graham once since that night he posed as the night nurse, a condolence call he made shortly after her husband's obituary appeared in the paper. During the call, it had taken all of Hannah's reserve not to ask him directly if her husband was in his lab.

How are you? he mouths as the others make room for her. His hair has grown out: each strand is long enough to coil and spring.

"If the George Zimmerman jurors can have a reunion, why not us?" Beverly says to no one in particular.

Hannah takes a seat between Jerry, the alternate, who is studying the cocktail menu, and Lana, the chemical engineer, who is checking her phone.

"Maybe we should have met at Nic and Gladys?" Jerry says.

"I still haven't lost the weight I put on during the trial," Beverly says. "Did you ever sell your story to the *Globe*?" she asks Jerry.

"My literary agent dumped me."

"Who's the lucky man?" Beverly asks Amanda, admiring the schoolteacher's ring.

"Joseph, the policeman assigned to protect me after I got those death threats. We fell in love."

Graham is staring at Hannah as if he doesn't entirely recognize her. And he doesn't. She no longer recognizes herself.

"Maybe we should go around the table and each say something about our reflections on the experience," Beverly says after they order drinks.

No one volunteers, so she says, "I guess I'll start first. Except for raising my kids, being on the jury was the most important job I ever did. I just don't get it. Why did people hate us so much? A couple of weeks after the judge released our names, I was eating with my kids at Burrito Boys and the manager asked me to leave. In front of my kids."

Lana speaks next. "It was a rewarding experience until I felt the judge undermined us. I thought fourteen years was too lenient. The crime was unspeakable."

"I still can't get that picture of the crib out of my head," Beverly says.

"Yes, the crime was indefensible," Graham says, "but sending her to prison was wrong. She should have been sentenced to a psychiatric hospital for the criminally insane."

He looks at Hannah when he speaks.

The waitress arrives.

Beverly orders the Seaside Trio, Amanda the Shrimp Your Way, Graham the baked sole, Lana the salmon, Hannah a salad and baked potato, and Jerry the Admiral's Feast and another mojito.

"Is the court paying for this?" Jerry asks. "The trial cost me big-time. My landlord towed my trailer away. I came back to nothing. All I had was the *Globe* thing. I told my agent to try to get me five grand. I mean, that's nothing to those tabloids. We were in negotiations. But then that girl texted her boyfriend to kill himself and I was old news. I'd rather go to jail than sit on a jury again."

The schoolteacher speaks next. "If it hadn't been for my fiancé, I don't know what would have happened. After I got the death threats, I took a leave of absence from teaching. I just couldn't cope. Every Sunday, a crazy girl with 'Silence for Caleb' written on her forehead and masking tape over her mouth stood outside my church."

Hannah's turn is next. She tells them that her husband died six weeks after the trial ended, and that for her the two experiences are forever melded. Hannah normally uses the word "passed" to signify what actually took place. His chemistry transformed into energy, and that energy passed out of his body. But today, she chooses to say "died." These people have seen the melted crib; "passed" doesn't cover it.

She accepts their condolences as she accepted the casseroles neighbors brought over, with gratitude but with no intention of eating them.

Graham goes last. "It took me a while to make peace with the verdict after learning what I did about the suppressed evidence, but I still believe that Anca is guilty. She may not have acted alone, but she started the fire."

"Was everyone as upset as me to learn that Tim had a record?" Beverly asks.

"One of the charges was battery," Amanda says. "The girlfriend before Stephana had a restraining order against him."

"I don't see what beating up a girlfriend has to do with arson," Jerry says.

"Neither did the judge," Lana says.

"But if you had known that Tim was violent?" Amanda asks.

"I don't like where this is going," Lana says.

"We're just talking," Jerry says, looking around for the waitress. His glass contains only ice cubes.

"How many want to take a re-vote?" Beverly says.

"What would be the point?" Lana says. "It's not legal."

"We would know our own hearts," Beverly says.

"I'm curious," Amanda says.

"Me too," Jerry says.

"As long as the votes remain anonymous," Graham says.

"I don't see what this proves, but fine," Lana says.

Graham resumes his foreman role and hands out napkins for the vote.

The jurors pass around a pen. When the pen reaches Hannah, she writes, "NOT GUILTY."

"Remember," Graham says before tallying the votes, "we did our best with the evidence presented. It was never our job to second-guess the law."

He reads the votes to himself first as he did during deliberations. "Five guilty, one not guilty," he says.

"Can I change my vote to not guilty?" Beverly says.

"Anca's eyelashes were singed, for God's sake," Lana says.

"Only a retard would use paint thinner," Jerry says.

"Please, can we eat our lunch in peace?" Amanda says.

Jerry stands up and starts waving his napkin to attract the waitress. "Where's our food?"

"Cigarette?" Graham asks Hannah.

He ushers her outside.

"I wanted to call you so many times," he says.

Hannah taps her feet as she stands next to him. She now taps her feet habitually. The electricity that passed out of her husband's body has been transferred to her. At first, she thought the impulse to never be still was the restlessness of grief, but over the past couple of months, she has come to accept that his energy is now hers. The ancient Greeks believed that the body was a wooden flute, the soul was the breath as it reverberated within the instrument, and the spirit was the music released from the wood.

Her husband's breath is inside her. It is his song that she is tapping her feet to.

She takes the cigarette Graham offers, slants it between her lips, leans into the flame. The tip of her cigarette is unsteady, and she has to guide his hand to light it. His hand is the first living thing she has touched in months. She doesn't want to let go.

Acknowledgments

I wish to thank the following people for their generous help with this book: Lisa Cohen, Amy Hempel, Nicole Holofcener, David Leavitt, and Ann Patty for reading early drafts. Victoria Wilson and Gail Hochman for their impeccable input and unwavering support. Terry Smiljanich for his legal advice. And my brother, Gary Ciment, for his anatomical expertise.

A NOTE ON THE TYPE

This book was set in Adobe Garamond. Designed for the Adobe Corporation by Robert Slimbach, the fonts are based on types first cut by Claude Garamond (ca. 1480–1561). Garamond was a pupil of Geoffroy Tory and is believed to have followed the Venetian models. He gave to his letters a certain elegance and feeling of movement that won their creator an immediate reputation.

Typeset by Scribe,
Philadelphia, Pennsylvania

Printed and bound by Berryville Graphics,
Berryville, Virginia

Designed by Cassandra J. Pappas